TERRA'S CALL

TetraSphere
Book One

P.T.L. Perrin

*To Chris, Vonnie + Family,
with love always!
PTL Perrin*

Copyright © 2016 by Patricia T.L. Perrin

All rights reserved. This book or any portion thereof may not be reproduced or used in any manner whatsoever without the express written permission of the publisher except for the use of brief quotations in a book review.

This is a work of fiction. Apart from well-known locales that figure into the narrative, all names, characters, places and incidents are the products of the author's imagination or are used fictitiously.

Printed in the United States of America
First Printing, 2016

Library of Congress Control Number: 2016902808
CreateSpace Independent Publishing Platform
North Charleston, SC

ISBN-10: 1530024196
ISBN-13: 978-1530024193

123 Mesa Street
Scottsdale, AZ 00000
www.FallingAnvilBooks.com

Edited by J.K. Edits

Cover Design by Ewald Sutter, Azar, Trostberg, Germany
Photographs licensed from Shutterstock.

*For Bill, my love, my long-suffering
husband and chief encourager,
and for my Creator, whose work I am,
and whose work this is.*

Contents

ONE 1
TWO 7
THREE 12
FOUR 14
FIVE 17
SIX 19
SEVEN 22
EIGHT 26
NINE 29
TEN 33
ELEVEN 34
TWELVE 38
THIRTEEN 43
FOURTEEN 46
FIFTEEN 50
SIXTEEN 56
SEVENTEEN 60
EIGHTEEN 64
NINETEEN 67
TWENTY 70
TWENTY-ONE 76
TWENTY-TWO 82
TWENTY-THREE 87
TWENTY-FOUR 90
TWENTY-FIVE 93
TWENTY-SIX 97
TWENTY-SEVEN 99
TWENTY-EIGHT 103
TWENTY-NINE 107

THIRTY	113
THIRTY-ONE	117
THIRTY-TWO	121
THIRTY-THREE	126
THIRTY-FOUR	130
THIRTY-FIVE	134
THIRTY-SIX	138
THIRTY-SEVEN	142
THIRTY-EIGHT	147
THIRTY-NINE	152
FORTY	159
FORTY-ONE	165
FORTY-TWO	169
FORTY-THREE	172
FORTY-FOUR	178
FORTY-FIVE	181
FORTY-SIX	185
FORTY-SEVEN	189
FORTY-EIGHT	193
FORTY-NINE	197

TERRA'S CALL

"Do you realize where you are? You're in a cosmos, star-flung with constellations by God. A world God wakes up each morning and puts to bed each night. God dips water from the ocean and gives the land a drink. God, God-revealed does all this. And he can destroy it as easily as make it. He can turn this vast wonder into total waste." Amos 5: 7-9 (The Message)

ONE

JEWEL AMARYLLIS ADAMS

Crash! The empty mug slips from my hand, shattering on the floor. Seconds later, the pantry wall slams shut, leaving me with nothing but questions.

I had come to the kitchen to get some hot tea and a cookie. The anticipation of starting school tomorrow had my stomach tied in knots, and I couldn't relax enough to sleep.

I set the kettle on the stove, switching on the burner to heat the water. I grabbed a cookie from where Mom keeps them, in a UFO shaped cookie jar that Dad made her when they were dating. They met at a UFO conference, of all places.

I was reaching for a mug in the cupboard, when I overheard Wolf talking to my father in the basement office. The secret stairs leading to the office are hidden behind a wall in the pantry, but they apparently forgot to close it, as well as the office door, because some of what they were saying could be heard very clearly.

I heard Wolf say, "The watchers told Sequoia it's nearly time. Things have been escalating these last eighteen years. Will Jewel be ready?"

"How? How do we get her ready for this? We have no idea what she and the others are supposed to do," Dad answered.

Wolf must have walked to the other end of the office because his voice faded and all I heard was "... the fate of the world rests on them..."

That was when I no longer felt the mug; only remembering it as it shattered on the tile floor.

I clean up the broken shards as quickly as I can, turn the burner off, and head to my room without the tea. One question reverberates in my brain and promises to keep me awake all night. What do I need to be ready for?

I crawl into bed and fight the sheet and blanket in my effort to get comfortable. Sleep eludes me. What are the watchers Wolf mentioned? And who are the others? What are we supposed to do? I wish I hadn't gone to the kitchen. I wish I hadn't heard any of it.

~~~~~

Dad was in his lab this morning—it's where he hides when he wants to avoid questions. Mom fussed over me, all the while pretending she couldn't hear anything I asked. I'm no closer to any answers about what I overheard last night. On top of that, I still can't believe my parents enrolled me in school. I don't understand Mom's and Dad's reasoning for no longer homeschooling me, but it's done and they aren't budging. It's my first day at Blue Mountain Mission School, and I'm already tired. Who can sleep with the world's fate hanging over them?

I can get through this. I repeat the words like a mantra in my head. The truth is, I don't want this. None of it. I want to go back to homeschooling. I'll try one more time to convince Mom to let me finish high school at home; as if that'll do any good.

The lunchroom is crowded with kids I don't know and probably don't want to know. I can't be sure, of course, because I can't see them clearly. I'm wearing one of Dad's inventions: a pair of glasses that dampen colors by limiting the wavelengths my eyes can pick up.

"Don't take them off, even for glances, Jewel," he'd said when he gave them to me. "It's important that you don't see everyone's auras and equally important that no one see your eyes."

He'd wrapped another of his inventions on my wrist and told me that it won't come off without a special code. I don't mind. The stylish wristband looks like a fitness monitor and I can use it as one. A smooth, hard face displays the time and date or, with a touch, can show the number of steps I've taken or how many calories I've burned. It's waterproof, weatherproof, and loose enough to wash under it in the shower. It's also so comfortable I can wear it to sleep. Dad designed this one to open a direct mental link to my parents. "Remember your Morse code, and contact Mom or me at any time. We're here for you, sweetheart."

Sure you are, Dad. Then why aren't you answering my questions – like why we moved from Asheville to the Cherokee reservation? Why isn't Mom homeschooling me anymore? What were you and Wolf discussing last night?

I can do this. I can survive lunch. I can make it through today.

A couple of kids vacate a table near a window that overlooks the courtyard. I take it and set my tray next to the window. The salad is better than I expected, with a variety of fresh, crunchy veggies. People leave me alone, which suits me just fine. No one is looking, so I tap out dash-dot-dot, or "D" in Morse code, on my wristband.

How's it going, sweetheart? His voice is clear in my mind. *Are the glasses working well?*

They're working, Dad. I don't see anyone's energy fields. In fact, everything looks quite dull. Is this how you and Mom see the world?

Not quite as dull, I'm sure, he replies. *However, we'll never be able to see the colors you do.*

I jump when a tray clatters to the floor behind me.

A girl's voice shouts, "Oh, Bullhorn! Paxton, come help me pick this up!"

Talk to you later, Dad, I say and quickly press the face on the wristband to end the conversation.

A tall boy sets his tray on a nearby table and turns to help a short fireball of a girl with long hair so bright that my glasses barely mute the red. He bends down and picks up the scattered dishes with no sign of annoyance. I would be annoyed. He wipes a strand of unruly hair out of his face. A cafeteria aide hurries to help with a broom and dustpan.

When the three of them clear everything up, the girl marches to the lunch line where some kids move aside to allow her to replace her spilled lunch. They're smiling, so she must be popular. Before I can look away, the girl turns and looks directly at me.

She has remarkable eyes. I can see them glow even through the glasses. I squirm, turn back to the window, and wonder who she is. The sound of a chair scraping the floor startles me.

"Hi," the redhead cheerfully greets me as she sits, uninvited, across the table. "I'm Sky, and I'm new here. One of the kids told me you're new, too. So what's your name?"

I shrink away from her and look down at my lap. It's been a long time since I've spoken to someone my age. Fourteen years, to be exact; ever since that incident in the park when I was three. Mom and Dad kept me away from other people after that, and I'm not sure how to act around other kids.

The girl hesitates and tilts her head at my reaction, then sits back, smiles and says, "Oh, I see."

What is she talking about? What does she see? Is she reading my mind? Peace washes over me. I can't explain it, but I feel as if my secrets would be safe with this stranger. I badly want to take my glasses off and really see her, but Dad's warning flashes like a neon sign in my head. *Don't take them off.*

"I'm Jewel," I tell her. Her smiling eyes are large and almond-shaped, like mine. I can see that they're blue, but what shade? My glasses prove to be effective color dampers. Mine are turquoise with flecks of gold. And yes, eyes can smile with or without the assistance of the mouth.

The boy (her boyfriend?) is alone at a table next to another window. He reminds me of a misplaced surfer, with tan skin in striking contrast to his blond hair. He openly stares at me, but for some reason I don't feel uncomfortable.

"Um, Sky, is that boy with you?" I ask my uninvited table companion.

She turns to look, waves at him, and then turns back to me. "That's my brother, Pax. My twin; my very tall twin."

"Why is he staring at me?"

"I don't know. Maybe because you're a girl and I'm talking to you?" she mumbles through a mouthful of sandwich. I feel more at ease with her and sneak another look at her brother.

Boys grouped at a corner table joke and posture loudly. Attention hounds. Of course, everyone notices them. Only one girl sits with them, next to a guy who seems to be egging the others on. She's not playing along, but she is staring at me. What's with all the interest in me?

Oh, great. She's up and heading this way. She walks, hips swaying, past tables and pushed-back chairs. Her gait is sinuous and draws the eyes of many of the boys in the room. I look down and hope that she'll glide right past us, but she stops next to my chair.

"Hi, Jewel," she says. "I'm Marla Snow and I've been assigned to show you around this afternoon. We share the next class together. Are you about ready?" There's a tiny sibilance in the way she says some words that disturbs me.

Sky gives me a blank look. Why is Marla ignoring her?

"Thanks, Marla, but I'll leave when Sky is finished with her lunch. I'll meet you in class," I retort.

Marla shrugs and walks away. As soon as she's out of earshot Sky whispers to me, "There's something off about that one. I can't feel her."

What a strange thing to say. I don't pursue it because Sky is frowning, and for some reason so am I. She turns to look at her brother, who grabs his tray and comes to sit with her. She visibly relaxes, and the tension I feel is draining away. Odd.

Pax is as striking as his sister. His large eyes are ringed by thick, dark lashes, the same shade as his eyebrows. I can't tell what color his eyes are, only that they're lighter than Sky's. I like the way his long bangs fall over his left eye, and I like the way he's looking at me. I want to see his colors.

"I'm Pax," he says. "Your name is...?" I nearly miss the sniff because it's so subtle, but I can tell he's smelling me. Ewww. I'm not wearing any perfume, but at least I did shower this morning. He doesn't look disgusted.

"J-Jewel. Jewel Adams," I stammer a bit. I haven't spoken to a boy in fourteen years, either.

Before we can talk about anything, the bell rings. It's time to discard our lunch debris and head to the next class.

The hallway is crowded with noisy kids banging locker doors and rushing to class. A boy as tall as Pax strides with confidence toward us. Pax greets him, and the two turn and head down the hall. Am I crazy, or did he have the same size and shape of eyes as Pax and Sky? And me? I notice his short, dark hair and the way it curls along his neck and around his ears. I think I'm experiencing sensory overload.

Sky walks with me to my next class, Advanced Biology, and I'm happy to see we're in it together. Biology has always been one of my favorite courses, and I wonder if being a science geek is hereditary. My mom has a Ph.D. in genetics. Dad is an astrophysicist and an inventor. I can't tell which he loves more.

We find two desks next to each other and take them. I spot Marla sitting across the room. The teacher, Mr. Abrams, explains our course of study, and I soon realize that I already know all of the material. It was the same in my first two classes, Physics and Human Geology. One of the benefits of homeschooling is that I have always been able to set my own pace, and for the last two years, I've been taking college courses along with advanced high school classes.

My hands are in my lap, and I tap the bracelet, dash-dash for "M."

Hi, honey. Mom's voice in my head sounds like she's standing behind me.

Mom, I'm so far ahead of everyone. I won't learn anything I don't already know, and I'm already bored out of my mind! Please, please get me out of here!"

There are many more things that you will learn in school than you can at home. Important things. Stay alert and observe. Interact with others. I guarantee you will not be bored for long. I can hear the sympathy in Mom's words, but I'm not comforted.

TWO

It feels good to be outside on a Saturday morning without the glasses that my father designed for me. I take a deep breath of the humid air and can't get enough of the vibrant summer colors. Hints of the coming autumn peek through the leafy shades of green in touches of reds and yellows. How do people live in the shadows all the time? How will I survive an entire year in school wearing glasses that turn everything nearly monochrome? One week down, many long months to go.

The swing on the porch looks inviting, and I sink into the plush cushions, pushing myself back and forth with a toe. I'm frustrated that my parents are avoiding my questions. If I approach them with anything, Dad disappears into his lab or spends more time at the observatory, and Mom always finds a way to change the subject.

Looking off the porch, the meadow grass is thick and rich in the lingering summer heat, alive with the life-forces of small animals. A squirrel stills, sits up, and sniffs the air before it resumes its search for buried treasure. A mouse scurries into a hole, while a red-tailed hawk circles above and screeches. Their bodies glow like overgrown fireflies. I breathe in the peace of the moment.

A wall of trees surrounds our property, cut by a path that leads through the woods to the twins' house. Sky is in most of my classes and we meet for lunch every day. It's only been a week, but I like her company. She and Pax don't look much like twins, the only resemblance between petite Sky with her long red hair, and tall, blond Pax being the shape of their eyes – huge and slightly tilted, like cat eyes. I see the same shape on myself when I look in the mirror.

High above the meadow the silver disk of my lonely Sentinel glows in the sunlight. Mom and Dad don't see it. Dad says it's cloaked, which makes it invisible to most people. The hawk flies below it, scanning the meadow for food.

I catch the glint of an aircraft over the trees to my right and look for it. The local Cherokee have a regional airport in that direction and often fly their small airplanes near here. However, this one isn't making any noise. Where's the sound of the engine?

I watch it clear the treetops and my jaw drops. I can't believe it. A second silver disk rises to the level of my Sentinel and floats next to it. Where did it come from? Why is it here?

A movement in the woods catches my eye. There! On the path. Is that a ball of fire?

Fire in the woods? Oh, God! My parents! My toe catches on the deck the wrong way as I lunge out of the swing and end up on my hands and knees. The door is only a few feet away. As soon as I get my clumsy feet under me and reach for the handle, I hear Sky's voice shout from the fireball, "Hey, Jewel!"

I turn to look at her, and she is aflame. Yellow and orange streaks shoot up through the glowing red nimbus of hair streaking behind her in the wind. She slides her bicycle to a stop in front of the porch steps.

"It's a beautiful day, want to ride with me?"

I have never seen an aura like hers. It ebbs and flows around her body in shades of indigo, purple, gold, and yellow. Her head glows like a bonfire, made more vivid by the brilliant red hair. Rainbows play over her hands like miniature ribbons of an Aurora Borealis. Does everyone at school glow like this? I wouldn't know since I never take Dad's glasses off until I'm at home. I'll remember to thank him for the monotone refuge they give me around people.

"Do you mind if we just sit quietly for a while?" I ask. My hands and knees are still stinging from the fall. Did she see that? I'm such a klutz.

In answer, she drops her bike, climbs the four steps to the porch, sits down and pats the deck next to her. I take a seat and we look over the meadow without a word. Silence has never bothered me, but Sky likes to talk.

"I didn't mean that so literally, you know," I say. "We can sit and talk, or do something else if you want."

"Don't worry about me," she says. "You feel calm right now. When I first rode up, you looked like you were scared out of your wits! How are your hands?"

Oh, so she did see my clumsy act. "About that," I start, but she stops me.

"No worries. I startled you, but it's a bit hard to understand how a little thing like me can be so frightening." Sky smiles and her eyes twinkle. Really. I see that they're deep blue with silver flecks, like a Carolina sky peppered with tiny sentinels. I glance up. They're both there.

"Sky, why do you think we have the same unusual shape of eyes?" The question pops out of a place where too many questions have been bottled up lately. I feel a blush rush up my neck and turn my face almost as red as her hair. Is it okay to ask something so personal? I have no idea how friends are supposed to act. That's what years of near complete isolation, outside of my parents, has done to me.

When I look at her, the smile is gone and she's staring at the trees.

"Jewel, is there any way that you're different from most other people? Other than being my friend, I mean. Why do you wear those glasses all day at school, and why aren't you wearing them now?"

I guess it's okay to ask personal questions, then. What does she mean by that "friend" comment? I've never seen anyone with as many friends as Sky seems to have.

"I'm a pentachromat," I tell her. "I don't tell anyone. My parents know, of course, and Mom ran the genetic tests to see if we could figure out why I see millions of colors most people can't."

She looks puzzled, "A penta-what?"

"It has to do with the number of color cone cells in the eyes. Most people have three types of cone cells. There are a few who have four and see many more colors than usual. I have five. I see a lot more than just colors. In fact, you didn't startle me, Sky, your aura did. It still does. It's like nothing I've ever seen surrounding a human before."

I wait for the skepticism. Will she take her bike and leave?

Instead she asks, "What do you mean by aura?"

"It's an energy field that people naturally emit. I see it as colors. Yours is fascinating, full of brightness and movement."

"I'm an empath," she tells me. "I feel people more clearly than I see them. A lot of people are empathetic and can be influenced by the moods of those around them. I'm that way, too, but I also have the ability to change their moods. I had to learn to control how affected I am by others, and to change the general mood of those around me."

"The kids at school like you. They sort of flock around you," I say. "Is it because you make them feel good when they're near you?"

"Partially," she answers. "I can't make anyone feel anything, but I can affect their mood by changing my own. When I'm calm and happy, others pick up on it and begin to feel that way, too. It doesn't always work, you know. Have you ever wanted to just hang on to fury when something makes you really angry? I can't calm someone who won't let go."

"So how do you keep from getting angry when you're close to someone who is?"

"Pax helps me. He isn't an empath, but he and I have this twin connection. Or maybe it's another of his abilities. He keeps me calm no matter what's going on. Before we moved here, we had some bad earthquakes in California. I was scared out of my wits when the earth heaved and things were flying off the walls, but Pax calmed me right down and I didn't panic."

"What else can Pax do that no one else can? You said 'another of his abilities.'"

"I like to tease him and say he smells like a dog," she continues. "He does, but not in a stinky way. He can pick up scent molecules we can't possibly detect. He sees better with his nose than with his eyes. I imagine he experiences scents similarly to the way you experience colors."

I'm suddenly thankful that I shower every day. A gift like Pax's would be brutal in a crowd. I can't imagine how awful a boy's locker room would smell to him. It's bad enough for normal people.

Sky must sense my thoughts because she adds, "No worries. He can turn it on and off and focus it when he needs to. If you ever need a bloodhound to find something, Pax is your guy!"

My head is beginning to ache. I had no idea there were other gifted kids around. How many are there?

"Sky, what does all this have to do with our eyes?"

"You really should ask your parents about that, Jewel. I have to get back home. I'll see you at school on Monday!"

With that, Sky grabs her bike and pedals hard down the path. That doesn't seem very fair! I answered her questions. Why won't she answer mine? It's obvious that she knows.

I look up at the Sentinels, but now there's only mine. Did Sky have something to do with the other? Do they connect us, somehow?

I head up the steps and reach for the door when a blast of sound shatters the quiet. I feel it in my gut first as it builds in a crescendo until I have to slap my hands over my ears and double over with the pain of it. Deep and mournful, the wailing goes on and on and I scream. Vibrations shake every cell in my body and I go down hard on my knees and pray that my eardrums don't shatter.

When it finally dies down, I can't hear a thing. I'm shaken and afraid to even try to get up. Are my ligaments even still attached to my bones?

The door flies open and Mom rushes out to grab me in her arms.

"Jewel, baby, are you alright? Are you hurt?" At least that's what I think she's saying. I can catch a word or two, her lips are moving but the sounds are fuzzy, distant. She pulls me off the porch and into the house.

"I thought we had more time." Her words buzz.

"More time for what?" I ask. Her arm around my shoulder tightens. She sits me down on the couch and turns away, but before she does, I see tears in her eyes.

"I'm calling your dad. We need to talk."

11

THREE

While I wait for Dad to come home from the observatory, I go to my room, sit on the bed and open my laptop to run a search on the impossibly loud noise. Who else heard it? News travels fast online and I'm confident someone is talking about it. Sure enough, reports are coming in like popcorn; from Charlotte to Knoxville; from Columbia, South Carolina all the way up to towns along the Kentucky-Tennessee border. People at the farther locations are saying the sky moaned. Closer in, they say it sounded like a giant shofar or trumpet.

I google "mysterious sounds" and can't believe how much material there is. I watch clip after clip of video recordings of these noises from all over the world during the past few years. Most reports say they can't find a point of origin, but it seems like I'm sitting on one. The epicenter for at least one mysterious sound is right here. Why?

My hearing has returned to normal and I rush to the front door when I hear my father pull into the driveway. Mom must have alerted him because his first words are, "It's time to call everyone together."

"Dad, can't you and Mom just tell me now? Who else needs to meet with us?" I catch myself hopping up and down with impatience like a little girl, and stop. It's time they see me as an adult. After all, I'll be eighteen in a few short months.

"Let me get settled, and we'll talk, Jewel. You need to know some things before the others get here."

Dad heads into the kitchen where Mom is chopping vegetables from her garden. I usually help her with the cooking, but not today. I go back to the open laptop on the bed. A buzzing sound draws my attention to my cell phone in its cradle on the charger. I had forgotten it even existed. My parents gave it to me so I could communicate with my new friends. I thought they were optimistic, since I didn't plan to have any friends. Sky was, and remains, a surprise.

I answer and quickly move the phone away from my ear.

"Did you hear that?" Sky screams.

"Yeah," I say more quietly, hoping she'll stop screaming. "It was loud enough to wake the dead. What do you think it was?"

She matches my tone and says, "I don't know, but it seems our parents know all about it. They're not talking until we meet at your house later. There's something mysterious afoot and I'm dying of curiosity."

"I found out that sounds like this have been heard for years all over the world. I wonder if our parents know what's causing them." I describe my internet searches and she's eager to look for herself. We hang up and I go back to my laptop. More reports are coming in, but there's no explanation and I'm getting hungry. Finally, Mom calls me for supper.

Mom, Dad, and I sit down to a delicious meal of roasted vegetables, black beans, and rice. No one speaks until we've finished eating. I help Mom clear the table and get the dishes into the dishwasher. It's finally time to get some answers.

Our kitchen is open to a great room with cathedral ceilings and too much space for our small family. A long breakfast counter separates it from a dining area dominated by a king-sized table surrounded by twelve chairs. More chairs can easily be added with no danger of anyone bumping elbows. A buffet marks the line where the family room begins. The massive room ends in floor-to-ceiling windows that look out over the Great Smoky Mountains. Since the back of our house sits on a sheer cliff, the view is spectacular.

We gather in the family room and I take a moment to try to enjoy the touches of autumn color among the trees. I love the way the sun brings out multiple shades and sparkles in the forest, and how it prisms in rainbows through the glass. Mom and Dad sit close together on the couch, and I take my favorite chair next to a pile of books I've been meaning to read. Dad clears his throat, begins to speak, and everything changes.

13

FOUR

"Jewel," he says, "this will sound like fiction to you, but it's the truth." Dad's eyes become unfocused, as if he's re-living the story. Mom reaches for his hand and grasps it tightly, a soft smile lighting her face as she closes her eyes and leans back to listen.

"You know that your mother and I met at a UFO conference in Arizona. We shared a fascination with the possibility that extraterrestrials might be visiting our planet. Still do, especially now that we know the truth. We were married six months later."

He and Mom share a look and smile at each other. I'm used to their frequent displays of affection.

"Analiese and I spent our honeymoon on a tiny island. We wanted to be away from the cruise ship tourists on the larger, better-known islands.

"The sunset on the first evening was remarkable. Fiery columns of clouds towered over the eastern hills, reflecting the sun as it dropped into the ocean. A dark storm edged the western horizon and broke the sun's rays into a fan of gold that seemed to reach into space. Smaller clouds, painted in the brilliant reds, oranges and violets of a tropical sunset, floated above the surf and drifted toward us."

Mom breaks in. "I remember the scent of honeysuckle and jasmine that permeated the air that night. I was surprised that more people didn't know about that beautiful place. Amaryllis flowers bloomed in pots that lined our balcony. Their magnificent blossoms inspired your middle name, Jewel."

I picture the little paradise island they describe. I can almost smell the flowers and imagine how the ocean waves must have sounded kissing the shore.

Dad smiles at her again, and resumes talking, "It was peaceful, and we needed the rest. I normally spent long hours working at the observatory in Boone, or buried in astronomical charts in my laboratory, like I do now, working up at Clingman's Dome. Your mom worked in a genetics lab in Raleigh, and was especially interested in genetic anomalies and the origins of humans.

"We were asleep when barking dogs woke Analiese."

"I got up to investigate the noise." Mom interjects. "A scattering of tiki torches lit the small courtyard below our balcony and the light glinted off of a looming metallic shape that hovered above the palm trees across the courtyard. All the noise came from the dogs. The object didn't make a sound. I still shudder when I remember the chill that raced down my back and how the hair on my arms stood on end. I called Charles in as loud a whisper as I could, afraid that whatever was outside might hear me. I was afraid to turn my back to it, so I backed into the room and shook Charles awake."

Dad continues, "A bright beam of light, apparently a tractor beam of some sort, shot out and hit Analiese. She was lifted up, and floated toward the object. I tried to get out of bed and grab her, but my muscles were paralyzed and I could only watch the thing take her away. Then I blacked out.

"The next morning, the locals were buzzing with tales of bright lights, saucer-shaped objects and an alien invasion. Some of the dogs had disappeared, and patches of burned foliage dotted the small island.

"Boats brought in news teams, and military helicopters landed and spilled out men carrying automatic weapons. Our little paradise was overrun with aliens of the human kind.

"The oddest thing is that we woke up together, wrapped in each other's arms with no memory of what had happened that night. Then eight months later, you were born in Boone at 12:54 a.m. on May third. When the other families arrive, you'll understand why your birth date is important in all of this."

"So, how is it that you remember all those details now?" I ask.

"It came back to us gradually." Dad paused for a moment before continuing, "When your mom studied your DNA and found a group of genes that aren't exactly human, we knew that something had been done to her on that craft."

"Ewww. You mean I'm part alien?" I feel the blood drain out of my face. My skin feels clammy and I suddenly have the urge to throw up. It passes after I take a few deep breaths.

"Not exactly, Jewel. Your mom was a month pregnant when this happened. There's been some genetic manipulation, but you're definitely our daughter. Have you wondered why your eyes are different from most kids; or why you have five types of color cone cells where most of us have only three? We've since found out that there's a purpose for your gifts."

"What purpose could there be, Dad? I'm messed up!" The fact that they were already expecting me on their honeymoon flew right over my head.

"No, sweetheart," Mom says, "You're perfect the way you are. Just wait until the others get here and it'll make sense to you."

FIVE

The doorbell rings, and Mom welcomes Pax, Sky and their parents: Dylan and Coral Fletcher. This is the first time I've seen Pax outside of school and without my glasses. The eyes I thought were simply a pale blue are actually emerald green with golden flecks that shimmer in the light. His deep tan contrasts with sun-bleached hair, streaked in shades ranging from platinum to brown. I know from Sky that they lived in California before they moved here, and I imagine him on the beach, or out surfing the waves.

A predominantly blue aura surrounds him; multiple hues of blue with orange and yellow waves that remind me of an evening ocean reflecting the sunset. A yellow-orange glow forms a halo around his head. Pax means peace in Latin, and he's well named. No wonder he calms Sky when she's upset. Just being near him calms me and fills me with warmth, and I barely even know him.

We sit at the table with our backs to the kitchen so we can see the mountains through the wall of windows. Mom and Mrs. Fletcher prepare coffee and dessert in the kitchen, and Dad and Mr. Fletcher stand by the window and talk quietly.

Sky doesn't beat around the bush. "Did your parents tell you about our eyes?"

I glance at Pax, who leans back in his chair as if he doesn't have a care in the world. "They told me about mine. Does this mean you're also part alien? Wait a minute; are we related?"

Pax says something not even remotely connected to my questions. "We looked up those sounds on the internet, Jewel."

"Dad suggested we check out a website dedicated to the Cherokee. It's private, but he has the password. That's how we found out that this reservation is where three of the sounds originated," Sky explains. "The first recorded sound came from here, the year before we were born. A second one happened last year, and this is the third. We're definitely tied to the sounds somehow."

Before we can discuss it further, the doorbell rings again. Dad opens it to Sheriff Art Green and Wolf O'Connell, two tribal elders.

"Where are Storm and Sequoia?" Dad asks Wolf.

"On their way. We can get started without them for now. Storm already knows."

The adults settle around the table and we all pour coffee and help ourselves to slices of Mom's apple pie. I'm expecting to hear a story like my parents told me, about how Sky and Pax came by their abilities. I don't expect what I hear next.

Sheriff Green swallows his last bite of pie and clears his throat. "Something is wrong with our planet, and you kids will have to fix it."

Sky and I sit frozen with our mouths hanging open, which is not very attractive. I didn't want to believe it when I overheard Wolf say something similar to my Dad during their conversation in the basement office. Now I'm in shock.

Pax straightens up in his chair and says in a smooth, calm voice, "Please explain what you mean by that."

I'm vibrating with nerves, unable to speak, and I'm amazed at the composure Pax is capable of. I'm growing more nervous by the moment. A ball of fear forms in my stomach. When I look at Sky, it becomes obvious why. Her face is paper-white and tears threaten to spill out of her eyes. Pax puts his arm around her shoulders, and I immediately feel the fear and nerves retreat.

Wolf stands up and says, "Art, you might want to lead up to that. These kids don't know anything yet."

Sheriff Green looks apologetic and starts to say something when I spot a dark shape rise above the level of the window. The valley is eighty feet below; there can't be anything out there. I jump up, knocking the chair to the floor, and yell.

"What is that!?"

SIX

The sheriff reaches for his sidearm and whips around to the window. An enormous black aircraft takes aim and shoots a beam of light at us.

"Drop!" he shouts.

The house shakes in an explosion of light that dissipates as it hits the window. Dad reaches for me, but Pax is already in motion, bent over and running toward the pantry at the back of the kitchen. He has Sky by one hand and grabs mine with the other, propelling us along. Mom has run ahead and is holding the door open. Sky's mom is already halfway down the stairs, while the men stay behind to fight. I pull my hand away from Pax's and look back before I dive into the pantry. What I see stops me in my tracks.

The light beam didn't penetrate the window and the men stand behind the table as if mesmerized. Sheriff Green has his gun in his hand, but isn't firing. The men look stunned.

The black shape hovers in front of the windows and fills the view with its bulk. It must be more than fifty feet across and it's made of some pitted, non-reflective metal similar to a stealth fighter. The front of the ship slopes up to a set of viewports and I get a glimpse of two strange-looking faces. Nozzles and a series of lights line the edge of the thing and a cluster of turrets sits on top, pointing toward the sky.

One nozzle that's aimed at the window begins to glow and Dad shouts, "Jewel! Get downstairs!"

At the same time, a flash of silver drops from the sky and slams into the black craft on the left, and another hits it on the right. It wobbles and I notice that it's triangular. Several turrets swivel toward the attackers. A third silver object beams a light down on top of it and it slips below the window. I watch the three aircraft follow it down. A fourth zooms into view and hovers where the triangle had been. At least as large as the triangle, its flat bottom and dome-shaped top are unmistakable. This, or one of the others, is my Sentinel. A row of viewports stretches across the dome and I see faces. These aren't strange at all. They have eyes like mine. It slowly floats upward until it clears the top window and then streaks away quicker than I can follow.

"It's disappeared," exclaims the Sheriff. I watch my Sentinel take its place in the sky as if nothing has happened. The other three that took down the triangular craft join the first. As usual, I am the only one who sees them. They must be cloaked again. Wait, four of them? I gather there's one for each of us, Sky, Pax and me. So who is tied to the fourth?

Sheriff Green and Mr. Fletcher run to the window and look down into the valley. The sheriff is on his radio, calling for backup. I hear him direct his deputies to the site below our cliff. It surprises me that he doesn't leave. Dad folds me into a tight hug.

Sky follows Pax back into the kitchen. Our mothers stand by the door, ready to scramble downstairs at the first sign of threat. Mom asks, "Jewel, is this what you've been seeing all these years?"

"Yes, Mom," I answer, "the silver one. You finally saw it uncloaked?"

"It's like the one that abducted me," she says.

The doorbell rings and Dad opens the door for Pastor John Clemente. I wonder what the school headmaster is doing here. Did he witness the battle, too? Without my glasses, I see the blue aura surrounding his body. It turns bright yellow around his head. He wears his light brown hair long and pulled back into a ponytail, at least what's left of it. The hairline has receded and left a large bald spot right on top. A flame flickers and dances just above that spot.

As soon as Pastor John is settled, a loud banging reverberates through the house. Someone insistently pounds on the front door. Or is it something? Are the attackers trying to get in?

"Storm's coming." Sky's voice is calm, but I see her shudder. Waves of rage and deep grief clench my stomach. I have an urge to scream, but I know Sky is projecting the feelings. She's anything but calm. Pax touches her arm, works his magic and both of us relax. Maybe I'm becoming more sensitive because this time I know the feelings are not hers.

"If it's anything like what we just witnessed," I say, "then we're in for some rough weather."

The twins and I hang back while our mothers head to the office downstairs. Wolf opens the door and a boy pushes past him and runs to the windows. I see him clearly for the first time. Bright red waves slashed by muddy streaks shoot out from him in every direction. I thought Sky's aura was wild, but this is like nothing I've ever imagined. It's more than angry.

This is the boy who's been hanging out with Pax at school. I watch him pace in front of the windows and unfamiliar electricity courses through my body. The soft curls of his layered hair are not black, but vibrant with streaks of blues and purples. He's tall and athletic and full of an energy that excites me. I hope his aura will change as he calms down, but for now, Storm is overloaded with rage.

SEVEN

STORM DARROCK RYDER

I can't believe what I just saw. It looked like the same ship that killed my parents. I was sure I'd see it crashed at the base of the cliff after those silver things attacked it, but all I see below is the forest.

Wolf puts his arm around my shoulders and tugs me away from the window. "There's nothing to be done, Storm. I'm glad you're here. We have a lot to discuss with the others."

I have an urge to hurl something through the huge windows. A stack of books next to a brown recliner rises a few inches above the floor, but I quickly set it down. I take three deep breaths, determined to calm down. The rage gathers and retreats to the place I've created for it, deep inside, where it smolders and grows hot and waits for the next eruption. It's under control – for now.

Pax comes over to me and lightly taps my arm. "Are you okay, man?"

"Yeah. Just great," I snap. He doesn't know my history, so I ease up on him.

"Thanks."

Wolf gestures toward the kitchen. "Let's all head down to the office. Sequoia will be here soon, and we can get settled and caught up until then."

That's when I notice the two girls in the kitchen. Pax has told me a little about his sister, the cute redhead, but I know nothing about the dark-haired girl beside her. She has the eyes, and must be one of us. I make a mental note to check her out later. Right now there's business to discuss.

We head down the not-so-secret stairs at the back of the pantry. Mr. Adam's office is the first door on the right. A mahogany desk sits at one end of the spacious room. It's surrounded on three sides by floor-to-ceiling book shelves and a wall of security monitors. A conference table and chairs takes up the rest of the space. Mrs. Adams watches the monitors and spots Sequoia's pickup pull up in the driveway. She hurries upstairs to let her in.

Sequoia brings freshly-baked cookies and Mrs. Adams places a fresh pot of coffee on the table. As impatient as I am to get some information, I'm thankful for the cookies and grab a few. Sequoia shoots me a look, and then smiles.

Mr. and Mrs. Adams share their story while we eat. I watch Jewel, who's obviously heard it already. Her large turquoise eyes and fair skin make a beautiful contrast to her long hair, the color of raven feathers in the sun, black and iridescent with dark rainbows. The colors shimmer as she moves, even in this light. My thoughts wander into dangerous territory when I look at her full lips, curved slightly upward as if she's about to smile. When she looks at me, she doesn't look at me, but around me. What does she see?

Mr. Fletcher clears his throat and starts speaking when Mr. Adams finishes. "Coral and I were in Alaska about eighteen years ago, doing some investigating of Inuit claims that the sun's position had changed and was causing a dangerous warming trend. My specialty is climatology, and Coral is a geophysicist, so NASA sent us as a team.

"It was a particularly warm November, and our measurements proved that the sun was, indeed, rising in a location several degrees to the south. The prevailing winds, normally cold enough to freeze the ice, had changed, and the warmth threatened the Inuit's way of life. It seemed the Earth's axis had shifted significantly.

"Coral had a second agenda, which was to find out if tectonic plate movement might be the origin of mysterious sounds being recorded all over the world."

Sky and Jewel exchange a look and nod at each other. They know something about the sounds.

"Fault lines crisscross Alaska north of the Denali Fault," he continues, "and small earthquakes are a regular occurrence there, which made it a logical place to begin."

Mr. Fletcher takes a sip of coffee and his wife continues the story, "We decided we might both find some answers in the Tartok Caverns, not far from the village."

"With our guide Anik, Dylan and I approached the caverns on snowmobiles that carried us and enough equipment to stay a few days, if necessary. We carried rifles with powerful sedative darts in case of a run-in with polar bears. Anik had live ammunition.

"He was the only one to remember the events of that night, and this is how he recounted it to us. As we drove up to the caverns, Anik spotted a bright light that shouldn't have been there. We took refuge behind an outcropping of gray ice and saw a silver craft float in the air in front of the cave entrance. The way he described it, it sounds as though it looked like the ones that attacked that triangular craft today.

"Three tall figures dressed in what looked like metallic jumpsuits appeared to be loading something into an open port at the bottom of the craft. They had no helmets or apparent breathing apparatus and all of them had white hair, but they were too far away to make out any facial features.

"They spotted us, scrambled into the craft, and maneuvered it right toward us. Before we could get to our weapons, they beamed me up into the craft and took off.

"The next morning, we woke up around a campfire no one remembered making. That day, we finished setting up instruments in the cave, but didn't stay to explore. I felt ill and wanted to get back to the village. The local doctor examined me and determined that I was about six weeks pregnant."

Mr. Fletcher continues, "We moved back to California when our project was completed. Paxton was born at 9:54 p.m. Pacific time on May 2, in Stanford, California. Sky arrived ten minutes later, at 10:04 p.m. In spite of their early arrival, they weighed in at just over six pounds and scored a ten out of ten on the Apgar scale."

"Their gifts became obvious when they were toddlers," Mrs. Fletcher says. "Pax was extremely picky about his food and hated going anywhere beyond the backyard. When he could talk, he often mentioned smells. Sky both laughed and cried easily. It seemed her emotions were all over the place until we correlated that how we felt seemed to be affecting her behavior. Children tend to be empathetic, but Sky's empathy was extreme. Pax was, and still is, the only one who can truly calm her."

Sky looks at her brother and I notice how blue her eyes are. I wonder if she's as fiery as her hair. Her generous mouth curves in a smile that warms me, but I quickly dismiss it. I'm cold inside and want to keep it that way

EIGHT

I'm not surprised that Jewel's and the twins' moms were abducted. My mom was, too, and Sequoia tells my story.

"My sister Salali and her husband Tom Ryder lived in Tahlequah, Oklahoma, among my people, the Cherokee. She was a member of the Wolf clan, as I am, and the clan adopted Tom when she married him. She was a meteorologist who worked at the local television station. Tom was a biophysicist, and he was fascinated by crop circles. He investigated the designs that kept appearing on reservation farms, and proved by the damage done to the crops on a molecular level, that they were not the work of hoaxers. He believed that extraterrestrials used the designs to communicate, either to us or to each other.

"When Salali was two months pregnant with Storm, she left Tom absorbed in work in a circle and settled under a tree where she fell asleep. A bright light startled Tom and he looked up in time to see his wife being drawn up into a silver UFO.

"People searched extensively for her, even though few believed Tom's story. He finally returned to the place where she'd been taken, thinking he'd search again for evidence, and found her asleep under the same tree. When she woke up, she thought she'd simply taken a little nap. She'd been gone for two days.

"Storm Ryder was born at 11:55 p.m. Central Time on May 2 in Tahlequah General Hospital, during an unseasonal series of severe storms and flooding."

Sequoia struggles to hold back tears, and Wolf picks up the story.

"It was obvious that Storm was different from the time he was a baby. His parents often had to snatch toys out of the air. While most babies soon learn to climb out of their cribs, Storm levitated out of his.

He began to use his abilities to gain advantage over other kids and had to learn to control both the telekinesis and his impulses. Tom and Salali taught him control while the tribe instilled their values in him.

"One day, when Storm was ten, Tom called us to say he'd found something significant. He'd made contact with an extraterrestrial and had information he could not talk about over the phone. He was bringing the family here, along with photos and a transcript of his conversation with the alien.

"They'd made it to our mountain when it happened. The police report said Tom had lost control of his car and plunged down a steep ravine with Salali in the passenger's seat. Storm was thrown out before the impact. I found our nephew in the hospital that night, clutching a metal briefcase as if his life depended on it."

I break in, "Tell them what really happened, Wolf."

"Tom did not lose control," Wolf continues. "Storm was playing in the back seat when a bright light suddenly flooded the car and momentarily blinded his parents. The vehicle lifted into the air, and Storm went into action. He opened the doors and attempted to lift his parents out, but he couldn't get the seat belts undone in time. He floated out his door and his mom threw the briefcase out after him before they plummeted to their death. Storm got a good look at a dark, triangular aircraft leaving the scene. It sped away…"

I know the story, but the memory of Mom's lovely eyes and sweet smile, and Dad's willingness to play with and teach my friends and me, opens a part of my heart I fully intend to keep closed. It does no good to remember happier times when I have to steel myself to carry out my plans. This time I can't seem to shut that door, although it's been years since I learned to bury my emotions. Sadness washes over me and pain threatens to turn me into a sobbing mess. What is wrong with me?

Then I spot Sky. Tears pour down her cheeks and Pax hands her a tissue and hugs her. My sorrow immediately subsides. So that's her gift. She projects her emotions. I wonder if she can read mine. I'll have to be careful around this one.

Jewel asks, "What was in the briefcase? And why the emphasis on our birthdays?"

Just then Sheriff Green's radio squawks. "Calling all units. Fight at Big Blue's. Shots fired."

The sheriff excuses himself and leaves in a hurry. Wolf stands up and says, "We've had enough for one night. We'll take this up tomorrow after church."

Pastor John also leaves, and everyone stands and stretches. The women clear the table and head up to the kitchen to help Mrs. Adams clean up. Sky and Pax approach me, but I'm in no mood to talk to anyone. I turn away and head up the stairs and out the front door. I may or may not be here tomorrow. I already know what the photos reveal, and Wolf has told me what the alien told my Dad. I want nothing to do with any of it, but it looks like I may not have a choice.

I kick my bike into gear and enjoy the way its roar shatters the forest quiet. When I reach the cabin, I turn on the news and settle in to wait for Wolf and Sequoia. It seems there's more bad news every night. Something is definitely not right with the world.

*****

Breaking News: "Hurricane Susan has intensified to a Category 5 storm with sustained winds of over 260 miles per hour, the strongest ever recorded in the Pacific. Evacuations are underway from San Diego, California, to Tijuana, Mexico. This is a massive and extremely dangerous storm, folks. If you've been asked or ordered to evacuate, please don't try to ride out this storm.

"In other news, a split in the earth has formed a miniature Grand Canyon on a farm in Arizona. Ten football fields in length and fifty feet wide at its widest point, the rift appeared overnight. Authorities are baffled as to what caused it, and they're keeping an eye on it as they're uncertain as to whether it will continue to grow. I'm Cole Porter, reporting for News Channel Six."

NINE

It's nice to sleep in on Sunday morning, but I know I can't make a habit of it. The pastor of Blue Mountain Mission Church, Mike Eaglefeather, is one of the tribal elders and Wolf's good friend. My aunt and uncle left for church after they told me we'd head to Jewel's house for another marathon information session this afternoon. I am not looking forward to it.

I wheel my dirt bike out of its shelter. Wolf and I restored it from the ground up after he surprised me with an old, broken down motorcycle for my sixteenth birthday. It's a beauty, even when it's covered in mud from one of our adventures. Right now, I just want to feel the wind in my hair and the earth under my wheels. I start the engine, kick it into gear, open the throttle, and head up to Black Bluff and the ceremonial stomping grounds. Lord, I could never get tired of this.

I feel close to God when the North Carolina woods surround me; as close as anyone who's furious with the Creator can feel, I imagine. I rein in my thoughts and concentrate on the narrow path. There are roads that lead up to the site, but I'm an off-road kind of guy.

The path takes me past the stomping grounds and pushes farther into the woods. It ends at a cave the Cherokee have kept secret for centuries. The opening is small and hidden behind ferns and shrubs. I dismount, hide the bike behind a large rock and cover it with branches before heading into the cave with my flashlight ready.

I'm not alone. Voices echo in the hollow space, and I recognize them. Great. My least-favorite people in the world have invaded my space.

"Well, well," Max's gravelly voice never ceases to irritate me. "Hiding from the world again?"

I say nothing. He isn't worth the wasted breath.

"Storm," Marla hisses. Every time she says a word with an 's' in it, she hisses. It's disturbing. I turn to leave.

"Oh, don't go," Marla says. "Let us show you what we've discovered. You're going to love it."

Curiosity killed the cat, they say, but I'm no cat. I want to know what it is. I turn and follow them behind a large stalagmite with its top half broken off and see Max's head disappear down a hole not much wider than his shoulders. He's wearing a miner's cap and turns the headlamp on. Marla climbs down a ladder and, as soon as she clears the way, I follow. The hole leads into a narrow passageway that slants downward.

We walk single file, careful not to slip down the steep path. I turn my flashlight off to conserve the batteries. Max's headlamp illuminates faint markings along the left wall.

"This is far enough," I say. "We don't have any equipment in case we run into trouble."

"Scared, freak?" Max taunts. "If we fall down a hole, you can levitate us right out of it. What are you worried about?"

Marla laughs and I cringe. I can't stand her voice.

"In case you've forgotten, Max, this is a sacred cavern, and this passage could be leading to something we aren't supposed to see."

"Exactly my point," he retorts. "We found something really strange a little farther on. You in or out?"

He has a point. I can use my abilities if we get into trouble. There's no way anyone else is down here, unless they got here first, and if that's the case, I'll gladly leave.

I lose Max's light for a moment when the passage makes a sharp turn to the right. By the time I round the corner, Max and Marla are standing in a cavern filled with lights. The walls, embedded with countless tiny crystals, reflect and magnify the little bit of light coming off the headlamp, and the result is magnificent, like a million stars underground.

"Didn't I tell you you'd love it?" Marla did a little dance. I swear I caught a glimpse of scales on her arms when she spun around, but that's crazy, right?

"I'm leaving," I tell them, and turn back to the passage. This time I use the flashlight and they follow. I have to get home and can't wait to tell Wolf about this.

When I'm out of the hole, I reach in to help the others. Marla winks, and it looks like her pupil narrowed vertically for a second. My imagination must be working overtime.

We walk toward the cave entrance when someone's shadow blocks the light. My secret place is turning into a busy mall. Whoever it is moves away and I'm the first to emerge. I can't believe it!

It isn't a person, but the shadow of a huge triangular craft hovering just above the trees. It looks like the one that attacked the Adams' house, and the one that killed my parents. Fury breaks out of its prison deep inside me, and I shoot my hands out in front of me and will the thing to shatter. My rage alone should have splintered it, but nothing happens. I mentally pick up rocks and aim for the windows. They bounce off harmlessly.

I growl and rock a boulder back and forth, willing the ground to release it until it does, and I lift it above the craft and hurl it down on the windshield. The rock breaks into pieces. The craft remains undamaged. I'm shaking with rage. Nearby trees twist and rip their roots out of the ground. I throw them like javelins at the windows, where they shatter like toothpicks. What is this thing made of?

"Get out here and face me, you cowards," I scream. A nozzle aims at me and fires, and I jump to the side to avoid the blast of heat that pulverizes the ground where I stood. A face appears in the viewport and grins. What the heck is that thing? It has a face like an alligator.

A dome-shaped silver object materializes above the hated aircraft. The triangle silently rises higher, picks up speed, shoots into the sky and disappears in seconds. The silver craft follows it.

I collapse, completely exhausted, and Marla comes over and holds out a hand, helping me to my feet.

"You should get that looked at," she says, pointing to my leg. From my right knee down, my jeans are in tatters. A nasty cut runs from about six inches below my knee and curves around my calf, just missing my Achilles tendon. Some of it is still seeping blood, but most of it looks cauterized. It's apparent that I didn't move fast enough to avoid the hit entirely. It looks painful. Why don't I feel it?

Max cowers behind the trunk of an oak tree; white, shaking and blubbering like a baby. I decide I won't tell anyone about his reaction. Heck. I feel like doing the same, now that the fury is back in its cage. From the looks of him, Max won't say anything either and I expect his incessant verbal abuse will stop. One can only hope.

Marla is the least affected. I wonder why, but that's a question for another day.

TEN

Sequoia smashes some herbs into a paste with her pestle and mortar. She has a food processor, but prefers doing her healing work the old way. I've never been happier that she's a highly skilled medicine woman. She's really putting some muscle into this mashing process, which tells me she's angry and worried.

"They're getting bolder," she says, adding another herb into the mix. "They know who you are, which puts you and the other children in danger."

I hate when she calls me a child. I stopped being a child when my parents died, but it's useless to argue the point. I pick my battles carefully where Sequoia is concerned. She's strong and stubborn, but she's also fair and has, on a few occasions, come around to my way of thinking.

"I'm sorry, son," she says and quickly smears the paste over my leg. I bite my lip to keep from yelling and try not to move.

The pain had held off until I reached home, but as soon as I dismounted and put weight on it, fire seared my nerve endings and the leg collapsed and sent me to the ground. It's a good thing Wolf was nearby. He helped me into the house where Sequoia quickly took over and cleaned the wound. I just about passed out then, and feel like I might right now.

My mind grows fuzzy as the paste does its magic. Auntie Sequoia is a magician. No she's an angel and I see her halo. The edges of my vision grow dark, and I'm out.

ELEVEN

CAROLINA SKY FLETCHER

I feel it as it happens. Storm's rage tumbles over me the way dark, fast moving clouds rush and roll over a flat prairie. It builds into a screaming tornado and the moorings of my own feelings begin to give way. A burning pain runs down my right leg and I know he's been hurt.

My legs grow weak and fold under me and I'm on the ground holding my head in my hands. I must have shouted because I hear the door slam open as Pax rushes into my room.

"Sky, hold on!" I hear Pax shout as if from a great distance, and yet he's right next to me. His arms wrap around me and I'm calmed by the sound of my brother's strong, steady heartbeat. Thank you, God, for Paxton.

"Pax, how is this happening? Where is Storm?" Pax's friend is nowhere near me; until now I've only been able to feel people in close proximity. "We have to find him. He's in a fight or something. He's hurt."

"We'll find him," Pax says. "Let's take my car." I love that about my brother. He doesn't hesitate to help me when I need it. He never complains and rarely questions.

Pax drives a brown SUV with four-wheel drive and special climate control. Mom and Dad do everything they can to make it easier on him, even though he's learned to control his gift. He's discovered a mechanism in his brain that lets him turn it on and off, but he's not one to turn down climate control.

We speed along the main road to the turnoff that leads to Storm's cabin. If he isn't there, Pax can follow his scent. It seems I can feel his emotions and might be able to track him that way, too. As soon as we pull to a stop, I jump out of the car.

There's his dirt bike, lying on the ground in front of the house. Pax sniffs. "He's here," he says.

I admit I'm a little miffed. We risked life and limb in our rush to get here. If he's safely at home, then what was that emotional firestorm all about?

Sequoia opens the door at our knock and invites us in. The large log cabin is modern on the inside. Open windows along two sides of a comfortable living room let in plenty of fresh air and light. A stone fireplace dominates the inside wall and carvings sit on the mantle. An oil painting of a Cherokee warrior hangs to the left of the fireplace, and an intricately woven blanket hangs to the right. On the blanket, strange-looking symbols surround a figure that resembles a pointed rocket ship with wings in a triangular shape. I've seen it somewhere before, but not in Native American art.

I start to ask her about it when I hear a weak voice calling from another room, "Auntie?"

"Excuse me, kids. Storm is waking up. I'm sure he'll be ready to join you, shortly. Please make yourselves at home." She hurries off down the hallway and turns into a room.

"Bullhorn," I say, exasperated. "If those feelings didn't come from Storm, who was obviously just taking a nap, then what were they?"

I get no answer, so I move closer to the blanket and examine the expert weaving. It is beautifully crafted, with a red, black and yellow background. The strange design must mean something.

My brother relaxes on the couch and I wander around the living room until Storm and his aunt return. He hops on one foot, using her shoulder for support. He is hurt after all.

Pax jumps up and helps Storm ease into a leather recliner. Sequoia goes into the kitchen and soon returns with a pitcher of lemonade, a plate of cookies, napkins and cups on a tray. After she excuses herself and goes back into the kitchen, the pitcher rises off the tray and pours liquid into three glasses. One glass floats to Storm, along with a napkin filled with cookies that have jumped into it from the plate.

The napkin looks like a mini-magic carpet and I laugh. I touch my glass, afraid it might float away, but it's just a normal glass and I take a drink of the fresh lemonade.

"What gives, Storm?" I'm glad Pax asks first, because my curiosity is choking me. What happened to him?

"Long story," Storm says. "The same thing that attacked Jewel's house just came after me."

He's about to launch into his story when Wolf walks in. He's scowling and I feel a deep anger in him. His wife rushes out and pulls him toward the kitchen. He stops her and turns to his nephew.

"Son, you might as well tell all of us at the same time. No sense in describing what happened twice. In fact, Jewel is on her way and I have something all four of you need to hear."

I sense Jewel's anxiety as soon as she pulls up to the yard. Wolf opens the door and Jewel heads straight to Storm.

"Are you alright?" she asks, and her concern for him washes over me. She looks all around him and frowns when she gets to his leg. I know she's seeing his aura, and it must not look great right now.

Storm nods and smiles at her, and I feel an unfamiliar twinge in the area of my heart. This is not good. Jewel turns her attention to my brother and me and greets us. She frowns a little when she sees my aura. I find myself wondering what color jealousy is.

Sequoia settles down in an easy chair near the fireplace, while her husband sinks into a leather recliner next to her chair. Storm relates what happened until he met the kids in the cave.

"I know Max," Wolf interrupts, "He's Sheriff Green's son. Who is Marla?"

"Marla came to school in January, last school year," Storm explains. "There's something strange about her, but I can't put a finger on it."

"Is she the one who hisses?" asks Jewel. "She was supposed to show me around my first day, but Sky rescued me." She smiles at me.

"She has a strange scent," my brother adds. "She smells like something we encountered in California. Do you remember, Sky?"

How could I forget? Something was in our cul-de-sac one day when we got off the school bus, just a week before we moved here. We didn't see it, but Pax sure smelled it. I felt no emotions from the thing, but it made my skin crawl nevertheless. I sensed it watching us.

"I do," I answer. "And I remember that when I first met Marla, I didn't feel any emotions from her. I thought it was odd at the time, but now that you've reminded me of that incident, it was the same feeling I had around that creature. Nothing—a void."

"Go on, son," says Wolf.

Storm continues with the story and I picture the sparkles in the walls and feel his wonder when he tells about them.

"I'm familiar with the cavern," his uncle says. "The crystal grotto leads to other passages in a dangerously confusing cave system. I'm glad you didn't attempt to go any farther. The Watchers inhabit the depths of the caves and they're the only ones who can safely maneuver them."

"Watchers?" We all ask the question at the same time.

He continues, "I'll tell you about them and the secret they guard when Storm finishes."

If I thought curiosity was choking me before, now it's really eating at me. Watchers? Secret? What is going on here?

TWELVE

Storm tells us about the laser beam that wounded his leg and describes how ineffective his telekinesis was against the alien spaceship. What else could it have been?

"The things we saw at Jewel's might have been stealth weapons the military secretly developed," Pax says. "Countries have always been in a race to outdo each other in weaponry, and who knows how far modern technology has come? Then again, why would the military be attacking civilian houses? And who would wear alligator facemasks to pilot an aircraft?"

"I don't think those were masks," Jewel says. "I saw something like that when I was little. We were at a park and I was playing on the slide. Mom sat alone on a bench watching me. I went down the slide a few times and looked to make sure Mom was still there each time. You know how little kids are. The last time I slid down and looked up at Mom, a human-sized reptile sat next to her. It had scaly skin and its face resembled an alligator with a short snout. It had a toothy grin and weird snake eyes. It scared me to death, and when I screamed, it got up and walked away."

"Didn't your mom see it?" asked Pax.

"She saw a friendly older woman and thought nothing of it until I screamed. Whatever that creature was, it had the ability to disguise itself, either through illusion or shapeshifting. When I told Mom it didn't have a rainbow, which is what I called auras, she panicked and a week later we moved to my grandparents' house in Asheville.

"I see through disguises; like those silver disks you saw attacking that craft. There has always been one in the sky above me and when I was little, I called it my guardian angel. Dad can see it on his instruments in the lab, but it's cloaked, making it invisible to everyone else.

"Since I've met you twins, and you, Storm, there are now four in the sky. We each have one. I call them Sentinels, and it appears they're friendly."

Jewel is calm as she relates her story, but Storm is growing agitated. I glance at Pax and wonder if he notices. His nose twitches.

"I wasn't going to tell anyone, because I thought it was my imagination," Storm says. "When we were in the crystal grotto, Marla twirled, and I thought I saw the light reflecting off scales on her arms when she turned. Later, when I helped her out of the passageway, her pupil narrowed like a cat's, but only for a second. Again, I chalked it up to imagination. Is it possible that she's one of them?"

"Dad warned me to never take my glasses off at school," Jewel says. "I will though, when I see Marla tomorrow. I'll take a peek and let you know if she's human or not."

Sequoia has been quiet during Storm's tale and the discussion, but now she stands and breaks her silence. "Wolf, they need to know about Tom's discovery," she says and points to the blanket on the wall. Her husband nods his assent.

"I wove this after Tom and Salali died, in honor of the two of them. This depicts the design of the last crop circle that Tom investigated. It was there that he met with one of the Star People from a silver disk; perhaps the one that took Salali and changed Storm's DNA.

"Photos of this design and the transcript of their discussion were in the briefcase Salali threw out the window the day of their death."

I marvel at the peace that emanates from her as she calmly talks about the death of her sister, Storm's mother. My senses reach out to Storm, and he's peaceful as well. I wonder if Sequoia is an empath.

She continues, "The Star Person explained to Tom that the triangular figure in the middle is the shape of one of the artifacts that were buried at the time of Earth's creation."

"It's a tetrahedron," Jewel points out. "Four equilateral triangles joined at four vertices. This design makes it look flat, but its shape is a pyramid."

Now I remember where I saw the design before. It was in a geometry book.

"Yes, Jewel, you're right. It is a tetrahedron, one of many that regulate the planet's functions. You can say they act as Earth's vital organs.

"When you get home later, I challenge you to research natural disasters that have happened over the last few years. If you're really ambitious, you can go back to the year you were born and see how they've escalated over time. That sound we all heard yesterday was an artifact's cry for help. The tetrahedra are sickening and when they die, Earth dies."

The room resounds with silence. Dread fills my mind with icy tendrils and my gut feels like it's crawling with worms. The dread flows from me to the others and from them to me. I send my emotions to Wolf and Sequoia, and hit a wall of peace. I draw it in like a deep breath. As I calm, the others visibly relax.

Pax takes my hand. "Does this relate at all to what Sheriff Green said yesterday? That something is wrong with the world and we have to fix it. Why us? And how?"

Sequoia sits down and her husband speaks, "Each of you has been genetically altered by the Star People in hopes that, together, you would be able to fulfill the ancient prophecy depicted by the symbols around the tetrahedron. You have gifts that will be necessary to complete your task, should you agree to take it on. The time and date of your birth is what made it clear to them that you four are the ones written about."

"Finally," Jewel says. "I've asked this a few times already. Why are our birthdays so important?"

Storm's aunt answers, "You were born during the Grand Stellium in Taurus."

"So what is that, and why is it important that we were born at that time?" asks Pax.

"The Grand Stellium occurs when the five inner planets and the sun and moon all gather in the sign of Taurus. It happens once every five hundred years. The constellation Taurus hosts the star cluster we know as the Pleiades. We Cherokee have always believed we are descendants of Star People whose original home was in the Pleiades."

"But we were born on different dates," I protest.

"You were also born in different time zones," she explains. "You and Pax were born minutes apart on May 2, Pacific Time. Storm was born on May 2, Central Time, and Jewel on May 3, Eastern Time. In fact, you were all born just minutes apart."

We look at each other in disbelief. We're almost exactly the same age.

Pax looks at Storm and asks, "Aren't you and your family Christians? Don't you believe that God created mankind?"

Storm gives his aunt a pleading look, but she makes no move to answer. He looks relieved when Wolf speaks up, "Yes, we are, and we do believe that God is the Creator of the universe and everything and everyone in it. That includes the Star People, the reptilian aliens, the Watchers and every other sentient race. We also believe Creator planted the artifacts on other planets as well as Earth in order to keep everything working in harmony. It's quite possible that the artifacts started to decline when Adam and Eve were tossed out of Eden and trouble began. The problem we have now is that we've reached a critical point and we're in imminent danger."

"Would the great flood have been a result of the same kind of imminent danger? With the exception of Noah and his family, everyone was wiped out." Pax has a great many interests, but I didn't know the Bible is one of them.

Sequoia explains, "According to our legends which speak of the great flood that covered the earth, a Cherokee family was also saved from the waters. We believe the Bible is true, but that more truth exists than can be contained in one book."

Pax is persistent in his line of questioning. "If the artifacts malfunctioned and caused the flood, then who fixed them that time?"

"Perhaps God released the Great Flood, just as the Bible says. Perhaps the artifacts had nothing to do with those events. There is no mention of them in the Bible, so there is no way to know. Mysteries abound in every culture. The prophecy is one of them, and all we know is that you four fit the description of the ones chosen to save the world this time."

"I have one last question, and then we really have to go. How does Jesus relate to the artifacts? He came to save the world, didn't he?"

"Pax, Jesus came to save the people of the world. The artifacts are the living organs of the planet. It's a different kind of salvation altogether," Storm's uncle answers.

I feel Pax's satisfaction and send it out to the others. We may not sleep tonight, but it won't be for lack of answers. We rise and get ready to leave.

"Wait a minute," Jewel raises her voice for our attention. "Who are the Watchers?'

"You will meet them next weekend," Sequoia assures us. "For now, concentrate on school and, Jewel, look at Marla without your glasses and tell us what you see."

It seems there's at least one answer we won't be getting tonight.

THIRTEEN

PAXTON HUNTER FLETCHER

Why did I feel the need to push for Storm's aunt and uncle to somehow reconcile Christianity and Cherokee beliefs? I'm not sure what I believe. The first time I met Pastor John in his office at school, he challenged me to read the Bible. I did, but it raised more questions than it answered. Now that I know about the artifacts, I can't think of anything in the Bible that's relevant to our role in fixing them. How will that even be possible, and is God interested in helping us do it? That is, if he exists.

Sky and I arrive at home without incident. The house is dark with the exception of the porch light. Our parents must have gone to bed. Tomorrow will come too soon for me. I fall asleep as soon as my head hits the pillow.

~~~~~

"Good morning!" Sky's enthusiasm makes me want to dive under the covers.

"It's too early, Sky," I complain, just like every other school morning.

My living alarm clock pulls the pillow out from under my head and hits me with it. I toss the covers off and pretend I'm about to grab her, and she runs out of my room laughing. I wonder if other sisters are as annoying as mine.

We usually ride to school in my car, but after breakfast Sky says, "I'll take my Mini today, Pax. You go ahead in your car."

I get in my SUV and follow her red Mini Cooper all the way to the school parking lot. Who knew I'd be watching out for alien attacks in the backwoods of North Carolina? I thought we'd die of boredom here after our life in Stanford. Turns out, a little boredom would be nice.

We park our cars next to each other and I walk her into the building and then look for Storm.

"Haven't you learned your lesson yet?" Storm's raised voice rises above a commotion in the hallway where he and Max growl like two mad dogs. Max's rough friends surround them, talking trash. Marla clutches several books and leans against a locker just outside the circle. She looks amused, until the books fly out of her arms and take aim for her boyfriend's head.

"Stop," I yell. "He's not worth it, Storm!"

The books drop just shy of Max's red face. The other boys disburse as soon as they spot the flying books. I can smell Storm's anger and Max's fear even with my scent guard up. Max turns and glares at me. He picks up Marla's books, grabs her hand and marches down the hall. I catch a whiff of Marla's strange and unpleasant odor, made more distasteful by her too-sweet perfume.

"What was that about?" I ask my friend. Storm's eyes look dangerous. I'm glad Sky isn't here to feel the darkness in him.

"Nothing. He was born a jerk and he'll die one." He mumbles something about getting to class and walks off. His leg must be feeling a lot better. I don't even detect a limp.

I shrug and head to my Physics class, the only one I share with Jewel. The thought of her lifts my spirits.

She sits in the row in front of me, two desks to the right, and smiles as I walk past to my desk. I picture the vivid turquoise of her eyes, now hidden behind her glasses. She bends her head over an open book and I watch, fascinated, as a wave of shiny black hair drapes to hide the soft contour of her cheek. Her scent, the trace I can smell with the scent guard up, is citrus and spice with a hint of honeysuckle, and my body responds. Not good. I really need to back off. She's interested in Storm.

Class is predictably boring since I learned it all in eighth grade. I'm taking an online course in quantum physics through my parents' university. Now that's an interesting field of study. My mind wanders to the artifacts. Do they fit into the laws of physics or are they more aligned with quantum mechanics? I can hardly wait to meet the Watchers on Saturday. Hopefully, they'll answer some questions.

~~~~~

Lunch is the highlight of every day here, and not only because the food is actually good. I enjoy spending the time with Storm and the girls. It seems everyone's noticed that we sit in the same area every day because they now leave one table by the windows free for us. A small school has its benefits.

Sky and Jewel chat about their plan to go shopping after school. Storm is mostly silent except when I ask him about his interests. His silences feel awkward, so I'm willing to draw him out even though I have no interest in motorcycles or hunting. We can't talk about the artifacts or aliens, but there is one thing we all need to know, and Jewel holds the key.

"Did you get a look at Marla?" Storm asks, keeping his voice too low to be overheard.

"I haven't seen her yet today," she answers quietly. "She isn't in the lunchroom. Maybe I'll spot her when Sky and I go into town later. I'm as eager as you are to find out whether she's human or not."

Jewel taps on her fitness monitor when she thinks no one is looking. I notice every move she makes and until now, I had assumed she was checking her steps or calories burned. This time she barely glances at it, turns her face toward the window and the corner of her mouth turns up in an almost-smile. Again without looking at it, she presses it and rejoins the conversation with Sky. I'll have to watch more closely. Something is up with that wristband.

The bell rings and we quickly clean up and go our separate ways.

FOURTEEN

Storm has some errands to run after school and I'm eager to get to the gym and work out. Kids mill around the cars; some talk and laugh, others argue and a few couples cling to each other and kiss as if no one else is around. Some walk with heads down, wearing an air of solitude. I wonder what color Jewel would see in their auras.

I see her and my sister jabbering about something while they fold into Sky's red Mini. She loves that tiny car. I hop into my SUV and drive home.

"Hey Pax," Mom shouts from the kitchen as soon as I walk in. "Dad's waiting for you in the gym. Want something to eat first?"

"Later, Mom." I head to my room to change into shorts and a t-shirt. The layout of our house is similar to Jewel's, but we have more bedrooms, and aren't sitting on the edge of a cliff. However, there are secret stairs into a reinforced basement, and our office is the same size as the one Jewel's parents have. Mom and Dad keep their equipment in the office. Mom monitors seismic activity and geophysical changes and Dad keeps track of climate change and weather events.

We have a full gym where Jewel's parents' laboratory is located in her house. It's fully stocked with equipment and training mats, showers and changing rooms. The four of us keep our karate gi there for a quick change if we decide to work on our katas. Sky calls them dance moves, but the movements are designed to mimic different fight scenarios. Dad's already there practicing katas, and so I change into my gi.

Dad has earned the Samurai title Renshi, which means 'Polished Master,' with the rank of Roku Dan or sixth degree black belt. He's been our trainer in Shotokan Karate since Sky and I were little. Mom and Sky both earned black belts and can hold their own in any hand-to-hand combat. Sky quit training because she couldn't get past the empathy she felt for her opponent. Every match left her depressed and wrung out.

Storm comes by a couple of hours later. Mom leads him to the gym where Dad and I are sparring and he watches until we're finished. "Is that Shotokan?" he asks.

"You're familiar with it?" Dad wipes his face on a towel and approaches him. "Are you interested in karate?"

"I've been training with Hunter Smith at Anikawi MMA. He owns the hunt shop in town."

"I've seen his operation," Dad says. "Mixed martial arts. I'd love to spar with you sometime. See how the two disciplines fare against each other. What level have you accomplished?"

"Third degree black belt," he puffs his chest out and I half expect him to beat it like a gorilla. He doesn't and I say nothing.

Dad continues, "In Shotokan, we call achievement levels Dans. You've achieved San Dan. Congratulations. That is quite an accomplishment. Pax will be testing for Yon Dan, or fourth degree, in January. You two should be pretty evenly matched."

I have to ask, "Do you use your telekinetic ability to get the advantage over your opponent?" As soon as the question has left my mouth I regret it. I should have known better. Storm stiffens and Dad looks outraged. One of the first things taught in karate is to act honorably in every situation. Without honor, the discipline is reduced to a street brawl.

"Do you think for a moment, son, that any tricks wouldn't be noticed?" Dad says before Storm can answer. "Are you questioning Storm's honor?"

"Forgive me, Storm," I apologize.

"Don't sweat it," Storm is gracious. "During training and competition, it's all me and none of my gift, as you call it. If I have to fight for my life or defend someone else, all rules are off and I'll use every trick I know. It's why I chose mixed martial arts in the first place. I'm going to kill the things that killed my parents."

Dad pales and I feel a little sick at his pronouncement. The pungent smell of bloodlust reminds me that I've let my scent guard down a little too much. I feel my own desire to hunt and kill rising and it dawns on me that Storm is an Alpha male, a powerful leader and motivator. If he decides to go after Jewel, I'll have to fight him for her.

What am I thinking? Am I laying claim to her? Since my nose acts like a dog's and I can smell pheromones, perhaps I've picked up on something she feels for me. Before I convince myself that she's my mate, I stop and remember we're humans, not dogs. She can choose anyone she wants.

Mom has supper ready when we've showered and changed. Sky and Jewel have finished whatever they were doing in town and join us. Jewel isn't wearing her glasses and I'm drawn in by the brilliance of her eyes. They're the color of Caribbean shallows around the islands.

"I'm glad the four of you are here together," Dad says after we've polished off Mom's chicken and dumplings. "I've had keys made to the house and I'm giving you the code for the basement. We have a fully stocked gym that you need to make use of, and I will be honored to be your trainer. We don't know what you might face in this quest of yours, and it's best to be prepared."

Jewel says what we're all thinking, "We haven't accepted the challenge yet."

"Nevertheless," Dad continues. "Whether you do or don't accept it, the training will help you to survive whatever happens. If we're near the end of the world, you'll need it as long as you're alive. Your choice might give this old planet a fresh start if you're successful. You'll need training for that, as well."

Jewel and Storm speak at the same time, "Thank you, Mr. Fletcher." They share a smile and Sky shoots me a look. She feels the burn of jealousy taking me over and pushes peace toward me. I take it gratefully.

"Please call Coral and me by our first names, and I'm sure that Charles and Analiese and Wolf and Sequoia will feel the same. Since all you kids are in this together, we need to feel and act like family.

"However, when we train, you should call me Sensei. Respect is intrinsic in karate."

"We saw Max and Marla downtown," Sky announces. "Jewel got a good look at her without the glasses."

"What did you see? Is she human?" I ask.

Jewel closes her eyes and I get the impression she's gathering herself to deliver the news. We hold our breath until we can't any longer.

"She's neither human nor reptilian," she finally says. "She's both."

"A reptilian hybrid. I'd heard of others," Dad's voice trails off. He clenches his jaw and his eyes have a steely glint. His voice sounds determined when he says, "Unfortunately, the stakes have gone up. The attacks will escalate, and you need to be prepared. You should be training here every day. When it's time, I pray you'll be ready."

"We haven't decided...."

Dad interrupts Jewel, "You may not have a choice."

FIFTEEN

We meet at our house after supper every day. Thanks to Pastor John's rescheduling of our classes, we each have a free period in the afternoon to get our homework done. He knows we'll need to make a decision very soon.

Jewel is the novice, but masters the first few katas easily. Under Dad's training, she soon feels confident and eager to advance. I admire her determination, especially when she winces in pain, or I catch her limping when she doesn't think anyone's watching. She's beautiful and tough, and I know I'm not the only one who's noticing her.

The rest of us use the strength training equipment, run the indoor track or spar on the mats. The days pass quickly, and tomorrow we meet the Watchers.

Since our folks have been tight-lipped about the mysterious Watchers, each of us has tried to find out more using online searches. Most sites referred to them as fallen angels or demons. One site named many of them and listed what they taught humans about astronomy, astrology and earth sciences. Are we about to meet angelic beings, or giant Nephilim?

~~~~~

I wake up before my alarm-clock of a sister gets up. I could turn the tables on her, but I'm a nice guy and choose to shower and shave instead. We should look our best if we're going to meet angels.

Mom and Dad decline to come with us. They want to hear all about it, but Sequoia had asked that we four be the only ones with her today. Sky and I take my car and meet the others at the sacred stomping grounds. It surprises me how much trust the Cherokee are putting in us when we haven't decided to cooperate yet.

Sequoia is dressed in jeans and cowboy boots. She wears a Native American beaded doeskin tunic with a belt of silver coins wrapped around her waist. Her long dark hair is in a single braid, woven with leather straps, that hangs down her back. Storm is dressed in black, as usual. The rest of us look nice, and I'm eager to get going.

We follow Sequoia along a narrow path to a clearing in front of a small half-hidden cave entrance. I spot the three beings in the clearing. If these are angels, all the pictures are dead wrong.

In fact, they're little gray men with huge heads and enormous onyx eyes, and they're dressed in gray overalls. I doubt these are the Watchers the articles referred to. It's hard to believe these little guys protect the secret of the artifacts.

I drop my guard and breathe. They smell of dank mold and cold rock. I scent nothing other than the smell of the caves they live in. Every living thing has its own unique scent signature, but these creatures have none. It's...disturbing. The middle one takes a step toward us and stops.

My head begins to buzz and fills with a voice that sounds more mechanical than from a living being.

Welcome, Star Children.

The others look as startled as I feel. It must have been broadcast to all of us. Sequoia remains calm. She's communicated with them before.

Please sit.

We sit cross-legged in a semicircle, Sky to my right and Jewel to my left. Sequoia sits next to Storm who leans his back against a rock and stretches out his legs. Maybe there's still residual pain.

The spokesman wastes no time. *When Creator made Terra, this planet you call Earth, he placed in her body the organs that were necessary for her survival. You refer to them as artifacts. We have cared for the artifact that was placed deep inside this mountain at the creation of the planet.*

Jewel speaks up, "Do you mean you, personally, or generations of your people?"

The Watcher turns to her but projects his answer to us all. *We are offspring of the Allaran race, those who pilot the disc-shaped craft you alone can see. When our time here is complete, they replace us. It has always been so. Our sole purpose is to monitor and protect the artifact.*

I ask, "Will we be able to see it?"

He turns to me. *When the time comes, we will lead you to it. It is ill and unbalanced, but the time is not yet right for you to intervene. You must prepare yourselves for battle.*

"Battle?" asks Storm.

He looks at Storm and then shifts his gaze to each of us in turn. *The Allarans are your allies. Their home planet Allara revolves around the sun Alcyone in the Pleiades star cluster. Their travels between your world and theirs have caused permanent passages that link the two worlds. You call them wormholes. What happens on Terra affects Allara. What happens on Allara affects Terra.*

The Dracans originate from the planet Draconis which revolves around a sun in the constellation Orion. Unlike the Allarans, they have not created permanent passages to Terra, but have developed a star drive that bends space and time. They came to Terra many thousands of years ago in order to mine gold and other elements from Terra's crust; elements necessary for their star drives. The fate of their planet is not linked to yours in the same way.

Allara has her own artifacts, but when Terra's became ill, so did hers. That is how Allaran scientists discovered that the artifacts of the two planets are interconnected. When Terra's are fixed, Allara's will heal. This is our hope, because the alternative is unthinkable. This is why the Allarans interfered in your development and altered your DNA to give you enhancements you will need to complete the task."

"This isn't the first time, is it?" Sky asks. "Were the artifacts sick when the Great Flood swamped the earth? What about when Atlantis sank and the great civilizations were destroyed? History is full of global natural disasters. The Ice Age. The dinosaur extinction. Who fixed the artifacts then?"

The little gray man fixes his eyes on my sister. *It is true that Terra has been troubled, Little One.*

She isn't going to like that. This creature is calling my sister "little"? She's at least a foot taller than he is. Sure enough, I receive a flash of annoyance from her.

He continues. *Terra has experienced many growing pains in her lifetime, but the artifacts did not cause the changes. They grew as well, much like the organs of a baby developing into an adult human. Growth is not easy, nor without casualties. You humans experience hormonal changes. As you grow, you discard what no longer fits, and take on increasingly complex ideals and tasks. Your emotions change from those of a needy infant to those of a mature adult. It is the same for all living creatures, and your planet Terra is the living host of all her inhabitants.*

The ancient civilizations you refer to were destroyed in a war between the Allarans and the Dracans. Creator allowed neither side to win. He permitted the Allarans to continue their vigil over Terra so long as they stopped interfering with human development. He also allowed the Dracans to inhabit Terra.

The Dracan starships were demolished during that war. With their means of travel between the two worlds destroyed, they built huge cities below the surface of the earth and sea. We believe their mining activities have resulted in sickening the artifacts by stripping them of their nutrients.

Terra was created to live until the end of time. This illness is causing her organs to fail, and when they do, both Terra and Allara will die. If you four do not take up this task, two planets and everything and everyone on them will be destroyed.

No pressure. "How do we accomplish this Herculean task?" I ask. "We have gifts, but we're not super-beings. How do you expect four otherwise normal teenagers to save not one, but two planets?"

You will have help, and you will have opposition.

"By opposition, are you referring to the reptilians, or Dracans, that keep attacking us? The ones that killed my parents?" Storm crosses his arms over his chest and clenches his fists. I see the strain of his effort to control the rage. Sky's hand gropes for mine. She's feeling it and can't help him.

Yes, and no, young Storm. Not everything is as it seems.

Storm grunts and Sky squeezes my hand. I know he doesn't like that answer any more than I do. The Watcher continues.

Both races are the "sons of God" your Holy Book refers to, who intermarried with the daughters of man. Together, they influenced the growth of the civilizations that were later destroyed.

"Are the Dracans and Allarans the ones people usually refer to as the Watchers?" Sky asks.

Yes. Very few humans know about us or the artifacts. Our people refer to us as the Watchers. You refer to the Allarans as Sentinels, Jewel. Are sentinels not also watchers?

Storm asks, "Are they the fallen angels in the Bible?"

Some civilizations called them such, and others thought of them as gods because of their advanced technology and the knowledge they shared with humans. Angels are an entirely distinct species created to traverse dimensions and play a role on Terra that is hidden from us.

Since the war destroyed their interplanetary spacecraft, Dracans have been unable to return to their home planet. They have become adept at disguising themselves, and many dwell unnoticed among humans. We now believe they are in contact with their home world and are determined to steal Terra's artifacts to buy passage back to their planet.

Again I ask, "How are we expected to stop them, much less fix the artifacts?"

You will not be alone.

At that, the Watchers turn and head back into the cave.

"Wait!" shouts Storm.

"Hold on," I call, but they ignore us and disappear into the entrance. Storm and I run to catch them, but the way is blocked by an invisible wall and we bounce back when we hit it, landing on the ground. I think I've bruised my tailbone. Storm rubs his shoulder.

The others stand and we quietly gather our thoughts as we head to the stomping grounds. Sequoia and Storm take a large picnic basket and insulated jug out of her car and we sit at a picnic table in one of seven shelters around a large central clearing. We dig in to cold fried chicken and slaw while she pours sweet tea from a picnic jug. We eat without speaking.

"Did you know about this, Sequoia?" Storm's voice breaks the silence.

"Some of it," she answers. I wonder if anything ruffles her feathers. She's like a deep lake on a windless day. "When the first sound rose from the earth beneath us and filled the atmosphere eighteen years ago, the Watchers sent a message to the Tribal Council. They told us then about the artifacts and that the day would come when four young people would be called upon to fix them. You were born a year later, but we didn't know you were the ones until Tom and Salali interpreted the prophecy. They suspected it might involve Storm as his gift developed.

"Dylan and Coral were drawn here last year, as were Charles and Analiese. The Watchers told us years ago to prepare their homes, so Dan Jones and his construction crew followed blueprints the Watchers gave them and built the homes in time for them to move in when they got here. Much of the technology in the homes is alien."

We again grow silent as we eat, each of us reflecting on what we've heard. There's a lot to think about, and it's obvious we won't solve the world's problems today. After lunch, we clear up and head to our cars. Sky murmurs something about taking a drive. Jewel looks dazed when she gets in her car.

Storm says, "See you at your house after supper," and hops in the passenger seat of Sequoia's truck. We'll have to step up our training if what the Watcher says is true.

SIXTEEN

STORM

It seems the joke is on us. Watchers? Those little gray creatures remind me of pictures of Roswell, New Mexico, where a spaceship supposedly crashed back in 1947. The town is full of replicas of little green men that look very much like the real things we just spoke with. They're nothing like the accounts of Watchers I found online.

This whole thing is getting to me, so I do what I've always done to relieve stress.

My dirt bike rolls easily out of the shed. The tank is full and I head up the mountain. Riding rough mountain trails is what I need when I'm restless and barely able to cage the anger.

I ride up the main road and look for the unmarked dirt path that leads up to my destination. Jewel's dad works at a private observatory on Clingman's Dome, and I like the view from there. It's a good place to think things through.

When I spot it, a strange urgency to stay on the main road grips me. I wonder if the attack last week has anything to do with my reluctance. I'm about to take the turn anyway when another strong feeling hits like a cold fist in the gut. The dome can wait for another day.

It feels as if I'm flying on the ground as I bank around sharp curves; and I love it. I feel the contours of the road beneath the tires. The wind feels good on my face and I take deep breaths of woodsy air.

Wham! A surge of pain smacks me in the chest and I swerve and nearly drop the bike. It happens again! I'm not having a heart attack, am I? The road curves and I spot a splintered guardrail. The closer I get, the more I feel waves of fear and pain and something familiar.

Sky.

It's Sky! I stop, lay the bike down in the gravel on the shoulder and rush to the broken barrier. Fifty feet below I see a flash of red. Sky's Mini Cooper balances precariously in a tangle of vines and bushes that keeps it from plunging into the river below. A faint moan reaches my ears, and I pull out my cell phone and dial 911 as I scramble and slide down the steep drop. Brambles tear at my clothes and my hands scrape raw on sharp rocks. Adrenaline surges through me, my heart races, and I move faster.

"Hold on, Sky!" I shout, hoping she's conscious and can hear me. I hear branches snap beneath the mangled car and immediately reach out with my mind to stabilize it. Telekinesis is like an invisible limb that I use as naturally as my own arms and hands. I feel the objects my mind manipulates the way a juggler feels whatever he's juggling.

The car landed on its passenger side and I see Sky slumped over the steering wheel, held up by her seatbelt. Oh, God. I open the driver's door with my mind, knowing that if I tried using my hands, my weight could send the car over. Carefully, I feel along the belt and release it, but she doesn't float out. She's trapped, and I hear breaking branches screech across the metal. I won't be able to hold it much longer.

What's trapping her? My mind feels along the length of her body and finds the crushed portion of the dash pressing on her leg. The bent steering wheel has caught her leg from the other side. If I concentrate, I should be able to lift the steering wheel enough to pull her up and out, but will I be able to keep the car from sliding into the river at the same time? The memory of my ineffective attempts to fight off the alien ship crosses my mind, but I dismiss it immediately. This is Sky. I have to save her.

I picture a giant imaginary mattress and shove it under the car in place of the flimsy plants breaking beneath it. Then I focus on the steering wheel. Metal groans and plastic cracks and it's suddenly on the floor by Sky's feet. I tug at her and she floats up and out toward me. As soon as she's in my arms, I hear the crackling of breaking branches, the booms of metal crashing onto rocks and a distant splash as her little red car hits the water far below.

I ease her to a level spot and check her pulse. She's alive and breathing, but I can't tell if she's hurt anywhere. Have I damaged anything by getting her out of the car? Her neck? Her back? When will the ambulance get here?

Her eyelids flutter just as I hear the siren coming around the bend. When she opens her eyes and fixes me with that brilliant blue gaze, I have the strongest urge to kiss her.

The ambulance stops and two men in uniform slide down the incline. The taller one carries a medical bag. The shorter, stockier man carries a backboard and plays out a rope that's been anchored to a winch on the truck. They wear EMS badges and a no-nonsense attitude.

"Stand back, son," the tall one says. They lay the board out and expertly strap Sky onto it. The short one ties the rope to handles on one side and signals to the driver. He starts the winch that begins to drag the board up the hill, but it snags in a patch of brambles. Without thinking, I lift the board so that Sky is horizontal and float it to the ambulance. The look on the paramedics' faces should have given me a clue that I would have a lot of explaining to do, but I'm oblivious to them; I'm too focused on Sky.

Sheriff Green's patrol SUV screeches to a halt, and he directs the ambulance driver to take her to the Blue Mountain Medical Center. He has a word with the paramedics and they get in back with Sky and take off. I feel sick and sit down on the gravel by the side of the road, shaking with shock. He plops down next to me. His SUV with its flashing lights blocks us from the view of passing motorists.

"Dispatch is calling her parents. I'm sorry, Storm," he says. "This must be really hard on you, especially considering what you went through with your folks."

That's when it hits me. Memories I'd long suppressed flood in and threaten to drown me. I feel the Sheriff's strong arm across my shoulders and fight to hold back tears. Waves of pain crash into me over and over again. I couldn't save Mom and Dad. When that thing lifted the car in the air, I opened all the doors and tried to float them out with me but couldn't release their seatbelts in time. I watched them fall and crash into the ravine. "I couldn't release their seatbelts," I say out loud.

Sheriff Green responds. "You were a child. You did the best you could. You released Sky's belt today. Think of it this way: you saved Sky."

His words motivate me to stand up and head to my bike. The sheriff walks to the back of his SUV, opens the hatch and puts the back seats down.

"Come on, son. I'll take you to the med center." I float my bike into his car and close the door. "Can you tell me what happened back there?"

"I don't know, Sheriff Green. I got there after it happened. Sky woke up just before the ambulance arrived. Maybe she can tell us."

"I'll question her as soon as the doctors say it's alright," he answers.

"Sheriff, what if she was attacked the same way my parents were?"

SEVENTEEN

Wolf is waiting outside the tall double doors when we pull up. He helps me transfer my bike to the bed of Sequoia's truck. I don't normally use my ability when people are around, other than the ones who know about it.

"I'll talk to the ambulance crew, Wolf. They saw Storm in action. I'll handle it," Sheriff Green assures us. He walks into the building and stops to talk to the receptionist. He says something and she responds with a laugh, batting her eyes at him.

"Dylan, Coral, and Pax beat us here," Wolf says. "Jewel and her parents are on the way." We check in with the receptionist who'd been flirting with the sheriff. Her cheeks are still pink and she smiles as she puts our names on a list.

Sequoia and the Fletchers talk quietly in a corner of the waiting room, where a couch and some chairs are grouped around a coffee table. Pax slumps in one of the uncomfortable chairs in the opposite corner, away from the adults. His body language says complete dejection. I drop into a seat next to him. "Hey, Pax. What's the word on your sister?"

"Thanks for saving her life, man." His face twists and tears threaten to spill. I'm familiar with the effort it takes him to pull himself together.

"She has some lacerations and they're taking x-rays now to see if any bones are broken. She's conscious, thank God, but they'll do an MRI of her brain in case there's swelling. I knew something had happened, but I had no idea where she went."

It's obvious that Pax and Sky are close, maybe closer than most siblings. "Do you two have some sort of telepathic bond?" I ask.

"Not exactly," Pax says and frowns as if he's trying to find the right words. "It's more like a knowing than actual communication. I know what she's feeling and extrapolate what she's thinking from whatever is going on at the time. Her empathy allows her to feel everyone's emotions, but as twins, we sense each other on a deep subconscious level, like the subliminal hum of electricity. It's so much a part of who we are that I wasn't aware of it until I lost her for a while today. God, I felt pain and fear spearing through me, and then nothing. It was like I plunged into a void filled with total darkness. I was terrified. How did you find her?"

Before I can speak, Charles and Analiese come in and take turns hugging Coral. They take seats near the couch and join the adults' conversation.

Jewel hurries over to us, her face streaked with tears. She throws her arms around Pax and hugs him hard, and then turns to me.

"You saved her!" I can barely breathe as her hug crushes me, but I'm not complaining. She feels really good. When she lets go, Pax sends me an annoyed look.

She takes a seat next to him and holds his hand while he tells her what he knows about Sky's condition. Satisfied, she turns to me. "Did you see it happen, Storm?"

"I was heading up to the observatory on the Dome, but something stopped me and I felt this urgency to keep going. About a mile from the bend, sudden sharp pains hit me in my chest and a wave of fear nearly caused me to crash. I know now that Sky was projecting what she felt. By the time I found her, the car had crashed through the barrier and fallen halfway to the river. The more I think of it, the more I suspect another alien encounter."

Pax jumps to his feet and starts pacing back and forth in front of us. "If that's the case, then we're going to have to stay close together from now on."

I'm a loner and don't relish the idea of being surrounded all the time. Admittedly, these three are growing on me, but I need my space. Solitude helps me control my rage.

Jewel taps on her bracelet, the way she does when she's thinking, or maybe when she's just nervous. "That isn't practical, Pax. Except for you and your sister, we live separately. All of us drive separately, and have different schedules."

She gets quiet for a minute and her face looks like she's wrestling with something. "What if we were able to communicate telepathically? We could call for help without relying on cell phones. Sky could have shown us what was happening as it happened, and we would have seen where she was through her eyes. We're lucky Storm was nearby this time, but what if it happens again?"

"Impossible," I say without thinking.

Jewel giggles. "You're one to talk. Didn't you just rescue Sky using nothing but your mind?"

Pax takes a seat and I'm glad he's stopped pacing. "You sound like it might work, Jewel. What do you have in mind?"

A doctor dressed in scrubs comes in and calls out, "Mr. and Mrs. Fletcher?" We leap to our feet and gather with the adults to hear his report.

"Um," he says to Coral and Dylan, "Mind if I speak to you alone?"

"Why?" Coral asks. "Is there something wrong? What's wrong with my daughter?"

"She'll be fine, Mrs. Fletcher. Her ribs are bruised, but she has no broken bones and no concussion. Other than a few lacerations and superficial bruising, she's in remarkably good shape after the accident. Please come with me and you can see her." He glances at us and says, "Only immediate family at this time. Sorry, folks. Once she's in her own room, you'll all be able to visit, one or two at a time."

"Let's go, son," Pax's dad puts his arm across his shoulder and pulls him along.

"Later," he says as they walk away. He knows we'll wait right here.

I go back to the corner, but Jewel draws her dad aside and they talk in a low voice. He's shaking his head and she's nodding. I can see that the conversation is gaining intensity. If it's a battle of wills, I'm betting on Jewel.

Wolf joins me and asks me to tell him what happened. I repeat the story leaving nothing out but my suspicion that an alien craft was involved. I didn't see it, but I'm convinced. Could I be sensing it from Sky?

It seems like hours later and I'm yawning when the Fletchers come back with Sheriff Green in tow. He must have been allowed to question Sky while they were there.

Coral is beaming and Dylan says, "Sky is fine and asking for you. They'll keep her in ICU tonight for observation, and will either discharge her tomorrow or move her to a room where you can visit her. She wants out tonight, of course."

"She's upset about her car. You know how she loved that red Mini," Coral adds.

Pax remains quiet and doesn't look at us. Jewel gives me a perplexed look. Something isn't right, and the Fletchers aren't talking about it.

I'm exhausted and suspect everyone else is, too. It's a relief to leave the med center and get home.

I'm on auto-pilot as I brush my teeth and get ready for bed. Fatigue overtakes me and I sleep so soundly I don't hear the windows rattle, and I don't feel the bed scoot across the polished wood floor as the earth shakes.

EIGHTEEN

Sequoia opens the curtain, singing one of her Cherokee songs. Diffused as it is by the filtering trees, the light is still bright enough to make me pull the cover over my head.

"Wake up, sleepy." How can she be so cheerful after yesterday? "It's time to get ready for church."

"What about Sky?" I ask. I'm eager to see for myself that she's not too injured.

"Plenty of time for that after church." I don't expect any other answer from my aunt. There's no getting out of it. I missed last week, and Wolf and Sequoia fully expect me to show up today. I usually don't mind. Pastor Mike's sermons are relevant and interesting and he can be funny, in a self-deprecating sort of way. He's one of the good guys. My problem is exhaustion; bone-deep, muscle aching weariness. I guess the crazy events of these past two weeks, not to mention the pretty intense training at Pax's, have taken a toll on my body. I wonder if this is what being old feels like.

When I'm showered and dressed, I'm happy to see that Sequoia has laid out a substantial breakfast on the kitchen table. I help myself to bacon, eggs, a stack of pancakes smothered in real maple syrup, and a tall glass of orange juice. My weary body needs the nourishment.

"I just got off the phone with Dylan," Wolf says. "Coral says it measured 3.9 on the Richter scale."

"What are you talking about?" I'm confused. Earthquakes are measured on the Richter scale.

"Didn't you feel it last night, Storm?" Sequoia asks. "The house shook and rattled loud enough to wake us. When I went into your room, your bed had scooted from one wall to the other." She laughs. "You must have been dead to the world if you didn't notice your bed taking you for a ride."

"A 3.9 magnitude isn't much to worry about," Wolf says. "What does concern me is that earthquakes are extremely rare in these parts. I wonder if this has to do with the artifacts."

When we have our fill of Sequoia's delicious food, I lift the dirty dishes to the sink, turn on the faucet, rinse them, and stack them neatly in the dishwasher; all without leaving my chair.

Wolf, Sequoia and I pile into the truck and drive a mile down the mountain to our church. The road is intact, with no sign of earthquake damage.

Blue Mountain Mission Church looks out of place, as if it had been uprooted from Arizona and dropped into this scenic, forested valley in North Carolina. The brick walls are plastered to look like adobe and painted white. Square bell towers, each three stories tall, flank both sides of the two-story sanctuary. Every window, every opening in the towers, is arched. We enter through massive wooden doors under a vaulted doorway in the middle. The balance and harmony of the building is pleasing, but my psyche expects desert while my eyes see forest.

It's dark and cool inside. The echo of voices greeting each other quiets when the worship leader takes a seat on the platform, a guitar balanced on his lap. Drums, flute, a bass guitar, and keyboard complete the band, and we spend the next half hour singing. After worship is done and the collection has been taken, Pastor Mike Eaglefeather takes his place at the lectern and we spend the next forty-five minutes hearing his take on the Bible. At least, that's what I normally do in church. Today, I'm fighting sleep. Apparently my near coma last night wasn't enough rest for me.

We leave quickly after the service. Everyone has heard about Sky's accident by now and Wolf and Sequoia's friends send us off with good wishes and prayers and assurance that there will be a feast at the Fletcher's tonight. In fact, the Fletchers will feast for many nights to come with all the casseroles these people are sure to drop off.

By the time we arrive at the medical center, Sky is being discharged. Pax pushes her wheelchair to his dad's car where she stands up to climb into the back seat.

"Storm!" she calls out to me. I grin as a wave of joy grows in my chest, and I know it's not coming from me. I curb my enthusiasm and walk over to the car.

"It's good to see you're up and going home, Sky. I'm glad you're okay."

"You're coming over, aren't you; you and your family? Jewel and her parents will be there. There's a lot I have to tell you." Concern takes over and the joy fades.

"We'll follow you home," I say and glance at Wolf who nods his assent.

NINETEEN

JEWEL

Sometimes, I think I should wear my glasses all the time. The rapid color changes in Storm's and Pax's energy fields make me dizzy. I'm used to Sky's aura changing with her moods because hers has always been like a fiery kaleidoscope, but the magenta streaks cutting through Pax's peaceful colors are new and concern me. They intensify when he looks at me; like Storm's bright red flashes intensify when he's around Sky. Do we make them angry? Is it something else? Seeing colors is one thing, but trying to understand them is another thing entirely.

We arrive at the Fletcher's house and Pax helps Sky out of the car. Her pale face looks like a raccoon's, with two black eyes, a bruised nose and swollen lips. She must have hit it hard on the steering wheel after the airbag deflated.

She's wearing a pair of baggy sweatpants to cover the obvious bulk of bandages on her left leg. The too-long pants legs are rolled up, but one fold is loose and the right side droops around her foot. They must belong to Pax.

He scoops her up in his arms. An unfamiliar pang of longing washes over me. We've been working out as a group every day for nearly two weeks, but this is the first time I'm aware of how strong he is. With his shirt pulled tight across his back, I admire the play of muscles as he easily carries his sister into the house. The yellow waves in his blue aura have turned brown. Something is off. I wonder what color my own aura is right now; not that anyone else would be able to tell.

Dad and Dylan pick up a stack of plastic containers someone has left on the doorstep. The Cherokee ladies have wasted no time in bringing food offerings to the Fletchers. They're a generous people who allow no family in crisis to go unfed.

Storm and his family pull up behind our car, and we head inside together. Pax settles Sky into a beige leather recliner and lifts the footrest. Coral starts an industrial sized coffee maker and cuts a cake she found in one of the containers. Mom and Sequoia help her, and when everyone is served, we gather in the living room.

Wolf gets right to the point. "What weren't you telling us at the med center, Dylan?"

Before Dylan can speak, the doorbell rings and Pax gets up to answer it. He ushers in a couple bearing food gifts who want to see for themselves that Sky is well. A few minutes later, the bell rings again. A steady stream of well-wishers comes by to see the Fletchers and leave food. Some pray with Sky, some just chat for a few minutes. Everyone mentions the earthquake and there's a lot of speculation as to what caused it. No one stays long, but it's soon apparent that our meeting will have to be postponed. It's just as well. Pax and Storm have been trading yawns back and forth, and I've caught a few of them. Besides, I need to get Dad alone to continue the discussion we started at the hospital. I'm glad when my folks take their leave and we head home.

It's still early, but I shower and throw on pajama pants, a t-shirt and flip-flops. Mom is in the kitchen and Dad has gone downstairs to his lab. Every time I enter the pantry to take the stairs to the basement I think about the wardrobe in C.S. Lewis's *Chronicles of Narnia*. Dad's laboratory is just as magical to me; a place where computer screens are eyes on the universe and inventions have the power to change the world. I need to see Dad about one of those inventions.

"I've been expecting you, sweetheart." Dad is at a workbench littered with tiny tools. He's wearing a band around his head ringed with a variety of eyepieces attached to hinged arms that he can select and use as needed. The lenses range from simple magnifiers to those that allow him to see at a nearly microscopic level. He put it together himself.

A wristband lies pinned to the table in front of him with its electronics exposed. "Dad, you're working on it!" I'm happily surprised.

He was less than enthusiastic when I proposed the changes to him at the hospital. I thought I'd have to argue my point, but it seems Dad has come to the same conclusion I did.

"I've been mulling it over, Jewel, and it would be a safety feature for the four of you. You have a direct link to Mom and me, and we have one to you and each other. A triangular link is relatively easy. By including everyone else, what we're looking at is more like a snowflake and many times more complex.

"I'll have to modify wavelengths and program more variables into the device. Your friends will want to communicate with their folks, as well, and each of them will need one. If the O'Connells and Fletchers agree to this, then Analiese can collect samples of everyone's DNA and I can begin programming."

"Dad, I'm sorry. I had no idea it was going to be this complicated."

"Don't apologize, Jewel. I love challenges and this one takes the cake. It occurs to me that with so many people linked up, we'll need a simpler code. You four, especially, will have to be able to connect rapidly if you're in trouble.

I hug my wonderful dad, thank him again, and go upstairs to say goodnight to Mom.

"He's at it again, isn't he?" She's curled on the couch and looks up from the book she's reading.

I nod. We hug and she holds on for a little longer than usual. She kisses me on the cheek and pushes up from her cozy nest. "I might as well get to bed, too," she says. "He won't come up for air until he's either solved the problem or realizes he's starving himself."

I decide it would be best to say nothing to the others until my parents have talked to their parents and Dad has a working prototype. There's no purpose served in getting their hopes up when it might not happen.

Another tremor shakes the house as we sleep.

TWENTY

Physics is my favorite class of the day, but not because it's interesting. I view it as a simple refresher course. I look forward to it because it's the only class I share with Pax. He's as bored with it as I am, which makes talking about it later amusing for both of us.

Today, it becomes obvious that he is lost without his sister. Sky stayed home and will probably miss the rest of the week while she recovers. Meanwhile, I expect I'll have to watch him mope. For once I'm glad I have my glasses and can't see his colors, but the reprieve will only last until we meet for training tonight.

I take my time getting to the lunchroom. I grab my tray, load it with a plate of salad, and sit at our empty table. It looks like Storm and Pax are both off sulking somewhere.

"May I join you?" I look up at the sound of Marla's voice.

"Sure," I say reluctantly, "why not?"

She sits across from me and unwraps what looks like a ham and cheese sandwich. She smiles and takes a bite and I picture those alligator teeth ripping the food apart underneath her disguise. I try not to watch her eat but can't seem to keep my eyes averted. My appetite turns to mild nausea, so I push my salad aside and wish she'd go away.

When she's finally done, she says, "I'm sorry about Sky. Do you know what happened?"

I mumble, "We haven't had a chance to talk about it." It bothers me that I still don't know what Sky's family is upset about. We didn't have time to discuss anything last night.

"Where's your sidekick?" I ask, in an attempt to make conversation.

"Max?" she asks. "Pastor John sent him on an errand along with your boyfriends." I bristle at her implication, but decide not to respond. What errand?

Marla chatters something about her classes and Max, but my ears tune her out almost as soon as she starts speaking. I interrupt, "What do you want, Marla?"

She snaps her mouth shut and stares at me. I'm sure anyone would be able to notice the hostile tension that surrounds our table, though it's hard to tell which one of us it's coming from. Without my sight, I can't tell for sure.

"I thought we could be friends, Jewel. Apparently not." She gathers her lunch and stands as if to go, but I reach out my hand and stop her. A line from an old Godfather movie in Dad's extensive collection comes to mind, 'Keep your friends close but your enemies closer.' I don't want her to know that I know what she is, and making friends seems like a better alternative to spooking her.

"I'm sorry. I'm being rude, Marla. Please sit down." With a little 'humph' she takes her seat again. I have many questions, like why is she here and where does she come from, but I ask her about Max and she's only too happy to talk about him. I can't wait for lunch to be over.

Storm and Pax are waiting next to my car when school lets out. "Where've you been?" I ask, annoyed that they were off running an errand while I was stuck with Marla. To be fair, it doesn't seem like they really had a choice, but logic plays no part in how I'm feeling right now.

Pax looks a little pale and seems upset when he says, "Jewel, we need to meet at our house right away."

"Pax will lead and I'll follow you," Storm says, his face just as solemn as Pax's. Now I'm getting worried.

Our little caravan makes it up the mountain without incident. Still, I can't relax. Something is definitely wrong. We pull up in the Fletcher's driveway and the boys walk close to me until we're inside.

"Come on in," Coral calls from the kitchen. "Eat something, please!" It sounds like a command, but I don't mind. I'm starving now that Marla is somewhere else.

I round the corner and gasp. No wonder she's ordering us to eat. The counters practically groan under the weight of lovingly prepared, donated food. "Jewel, Storm, you'll both have to take some of this home with you when you leave. We couldn't possibly finish it all."

We help ourselves to plates of deviled eggs and chicken salad. I reach for a leg of cold fried chicken and heap baked beans and coleslaw on my plate. To my happy surprise, cold baked beans taste wonderful. I thank God I live in a community of great cooks.

The boys sit at the table close to the food. They can put away a lot of it at one sitting. Sky is in the same chair we left her in last night with a loaded tray table next to her. "Jewel!" she calls out around a mouthful of slaw. "Sit next to me!"

I drag a chair from the dining room and share her tray table. We eat in silence for about three minutes, until the words she's been holding back all day begin to pour out of her. The poor girl needs to speak.

"How was school? Did you have lunch with Storm and Pax? Are people asking about me?"

I grin, still chewing on chicken, and she laughs. "I guess I should give you a chance to speak." I really missed her today. The week is going to crawl by without her cheery presence and ability to lift everyone's mood.

"First tell me how you're feeling, Sky," I say and take another bite. This food is delicious.

"Sequoia has been working her Cherokee magic on me," she lifts her pants leg and I see the bandages are gone. "She rubbed some spicy smelling potion on my leg and face and they don't hurt at all anymore. It still hurts to laugh, though."

The bruises around her eyes have turned a nasty shade of yellow-green. It usually takes about a week for the black and blue to fade to that shade. Her nose is slightly red, but the bruise there is nearly gone. The healing process has accelerated under Sequoia's care.

"Sequoia could teach our modern doctors a thing or two about healing," I note.

"Dad says I have to stay home one more day, but then I can return to school."

"I am so glad to hear that, Sky! It isn't the same without you, and I miss you, even if it's only been one day."

We reach across the table and clasp hands and it doesn't feel the least bit awkward.

Dylan comes in and calls the boys into the living room. They bring their plates and cups along and settle on the couch. Maybe now I'll find out what's bothering everyone.

"The story we told at the medical center about Sky's accident isn't the entire story, as you've probably deduced," he says.

Storm looks at me, and I'm guessing he already knows what's coming.

Dylan continues, "There were no other cars along the stretch of dangerous curves when a bright light shone into Sky's windshield and blinded her. The same thing happened to Storm's folks, and you saw it when that craft attacked your house, Jewel. By the time she could see again, the car had crashed through the guardrail and tumbled and rolled onto those bushes where you found it, Storm."

I ask the obvious because I want it clarified. "So, was it another Dracan attack?"

"We don't know for sure, Jewel. When Sky regained her sight, she saw a silver craft hovering above the river on a level with her car. She didn't see any sign of the triangular craft that attacked you and Storm. Afterwards she lost consciousness and didn't come to until Storm rescued her."

Oh, no. That's not possible. The Sentinels? They're the good guys, aren't they? The thought that the Allarans might be our enemies tumbles around my brain and twists it into knots. Nothing makes sense, and my head hurts nearly as much as my heart. My Sentinel?

Pax breaks in and I feel some of the knots begin to unravel, "What if the Allarans didn't attack her? It's possible that the Dracans were the aggressors and the Allarans fought them off the way they did at Jewel's house. Maybe that one stayed behind to make sure she was okay."

"They're still guarding us," I add, glad that Pax spoke up. "Three of them were over the school, and when we got here, I saw all four in the sky over your house. I can't imagine they'd still be there if they meant us harm."

"I like to think that's what happened," Dylan says. "The problem is that we don't know for sure. What do we know about them? Jewel, you've seen a disk in the sky for as long as you can remember. We saw them attack the ship that attacked us. I want to trust them, but we actually have no understanding of their objective here."

"The Watchers called them our allies," Storm reminds us.

"And what do we know of the Watchers?" Dylan asks. "We simply don't have enough information to make a judgment call. I say we have to be exceedingly careful, and suspicious at this point. We know the Dracans are determined to hurt you kids, and it's possible that the Allarans are also hostile."

I hate to think that my Sentinel could be hostile, but Dylan's right. Didn't the silver ships abduct our mothers and mess with us while we were still in the womb? Was that the act of allies, or do they have a more sinister plan?

Training helps clear my mind simply because I have no energy left to think. Sensei works us hard today while Sky watches from her spot on a pile of mats in the corner. It isn't until after we've gone home and I'm ready for bed that I remember I never got an answer about the boys' mysterious errand.

In spite of my exhaustion, I have trouble sleeping, and get up to watch the news with Mom. It isn't good.

*****

Breaking News: "Moments ago, a magnitude 7.5 earthquake rocked the Northeast, sending residents running into the streets. The extent of damage and casualties is not known at this time. We will keep you updated.

"In other news, the remnants of Hurricane Susan are sweeping across the western states in a line of devastating storms that have dropped up to two feet of rain in some drought-stricken areas. Flash floods have wiped out entire communities. Fifty-five people have lost their lives and the death toll is expected to rise as these storms march across the Midwest. - Cayla Knox reporting for News Channel Twelve."

*****

It seems at least one major cataclysm happens every single day, and that's just in our country. World news is much worse. Thankfully, by the time the newscast is over, I'm too tired to think about anything and I'm out like a light as soon as I crawl into bed.

TWENTY-ONE

The quake shakes me to the floor. My alarm clock reads 4:32 a.m., and I know I won't get back to sleep. I slept through the other tremors, but this one scares me. Is the artifact causing this?

When Sequoia challenged us to research whether the occurrence of natural disasters has increased since we were born, I started with my birth year and began to read the reports. By the time I'd read about ten years' worth, I was convinced that what she said was true. The world is falling apart.

Does this mean we four kids, with no experience and no clue as to how to go about doing it, are expected to fix the problem? If we somehow manage to repair the tetrahedron, will the disasters stop? Will the earthquakes stop? What if they don't?

I wish Sky was going to be at school today, but her parents made it clear she needs another day at home. I don't blame her, of course, but I do miss her.

~~~~~

Pax is a bit more cheerful in Physics today. He winks as he walks past my desk to take his seat behind me, and sudden warmth fills my body. Even with my glasses on he's gorgeous. When Sky is around I have mostly sisterly feelings for him, probably as a reflection of the way she feels. In this class, it's different. I have feelings for him, but my thoughts are not sisterly at all. I remember the way his muscles moved as he carried his sister into the house, and how quick and supple he is sparring with his dad or Storm, and I feel a blush rising up my neck.

I check to make sure I haven't accidentally linked with Mom or Dad since my tapping on the wristband has become a habit. It's a relief to know they're safely out of my thoughts at the moment.

When lunchtime finally rolls around I'm reluctant to go to the cafeteria. What if the boys aren't there? What if I have to pretend to like Marla again? My hunger wins out and I'm happy to see that Pax is already seated at our table. When I sit down across from him, he smiles. Something inside of me flutters.

"Where's Storm?" A tiny cloud seems to come across his face when I ask.

"Running errands," he answers, looking at the sandwich in his hands.

"What kind of errands?" I'm really curious now. Yesterday he and Storm were both out, and with Max, no less. Neither of them could stand to be around the loudmouth, and yet they were running errands together, whatever that means.

"It's nothing to be concerned about," he says and avoids my eyes, but of course this only increases my curiosity. "Pastor John needed us to do something in town and we did."

"What was it?" I press. I may have gone too far, though, because he starts cleaning up.

"Nothing," he says and stands up. "I'll see you after school." He walks away and I'm seething. What was that? He's never just walked away in the middle of lunch period before. Something is definitely up, and I resolve to find out what it is.

Before I can move, Marla slithers into the seat Pax just vacated. Great.

"What's up with him?" she asks.

"He's probably still upset about his sister," I answer. Maybe that's it. It's time to change the subject. "Where's Max?"

"He's off with Storm again. If I didn't know better, I'd think they're becoming best friends." We both laugh at that. They can barely stand each other. There's nothing like shared laughter to relax the atmosphere. I decide to jump off a figurative ledge.

"Tell me about yourself, Marla. How long have you lived here?"

"Mom and I moved here last January."

"Where did you live before?"

"Raleigh. Now it's my turn for questions." Uh, oh. From the way she talked about Max non-stop yesterday, I assumed she'd be more than happy to talk about herself. I guess I misjudged.

"Jewel," she says. "What are you and your friends up to?"

I gather my lunch, stand up and say "Bell's about to ring, Marla. Enjoy the rest of your day." I leave her sitting there with a smirk on her face. So much for trying to draw her out.

I don't expect to see Pax again until after school, but he's waiting for me in the hall.

"Your curiosity is going to get you in trouble someday, Jewel." He looks serious. "You want to know what Storm is doing?" He grabs my hand. "Come on and I'll show you."

He pulls me along the corridor and out the double doors that open to the courtyard. We cross it and march along the breezeway to the parking lot. Pax has a firm grip on my hand and I have to practically run to keep up with his long strides.

"Where are we going?" I demand. "We can't just leave school!"

"We're running an errand, Jewel. I've cleared it with Pastor John. You're involved and you're coming with us."

I haven't seen this no-nonsense side of Paxton Fletcher before, and I must admit I like it. He holds the passenger door open as I climb into his SUV and buckle in. I take the glasses off, but probably should have left them on. Now I can't seem to keep my eyes off him as he crosses in front of the car and climbs into his seat. His normally calm blue and yellow aura is flashing with red and streaks of dark blue. I really need to find out what the colors mean. They disturb me.

"So, what's all the secrecy for?" I ask. "Does it have to do with our friends or enemies in the sky?"

"Earthquakes," he says. I wait, but he keeps his mouth shut.

"What about them?" I ask. If he wants me to quit asking questions, he'll have to be more forthcoming.

"You'll see." I doubt I'll get any more out of him for now, so I sit back and watch the passing scenery. We drive a few miles along the one main road through the reservation, and then turn onto a paved narrow road leading through a tunnel of trees, around sharp curves and up the mountain. We continue to climb through thick forest until we reach a meadow with a huge house smack in the middle. We park in a circular driveway in front, behind Storm's bike and a blue car that must belong to Max. I can see why the people who live here picked this mountaintop to build their mansion on. The view is breathtaking, no matter where you look.

"Who lives here?" I ask. Pax must be tired of all my questions, but how else am I going to learn anything?

"Chief James O'Brian and his family," he answers. "He's the Principal Chief of the Cherokee Nation in this part of the country. He's also a lawyer. A good one."

My parents and I had met him and the other Tribal Council members when we first moved here. They've certainly smoothed the way for us and for the Fletchers to make our home here. I wonder if they'll kick us out if we decide not to take up their challenge to save the whole world.

Pax grabs my hand again, and I feel a warm current start where his palm grips mine. It travels up my arm and through my body. A magenta glow surrounds our joined hands. Interesting.

He tugs me along, but walks slower this time, and I spot Max crouching in the field and holding a shovel. Is he digging a hole? Where's Storm?

Two patrol SUVs are also in the field, one with its back-end to Max and what looks like a rope attached to a winch. A deputy sits on a folding stool next to the winch. He's eating a sandwich. Someone in the far vehicle is talking into a radio.

Max turns to us and shouts, "Come to help or to bother us?" He's as obnoxious as ever.

As we get closer, I see that the rope is actually a thick cable that disappears down a large perfectly round hole. The cable jerks and the deputy starts the winch. I watch as Storm slowly emerges from the hole, hanging from a safety harness attached to the cable. He wears a miner's lamp and dusty yellow coveralls, similar to a fireman's getup.

"How deep?" the deputy asks.

"About sixty feet," Storm says. "The walls are smooth all the way down. Whatever made it stopped at bedrock."

The second deputy strolls over with his hands stuffed casually in his pockets. "Same as the other two," he comments. "The one we found in the woods behind Rob Townsend's place and the hole on Wild Bill's property were deeper, but they both bottomed out on rock, just the same."

Three holes? I'm beginning to understand what Pax meant by earthquakes.

"Did the earthquakes cause these holes?" I ask.

Storm answers, "It's more like whatever dug the holes caused the earthquakes."

He peels off the coveralls and hands them and the headlamp to the deputy who'd been manning the winch. Max joins us and we walk back to our vehicles.

"Any idea what's doing this?" he asks. "Let me rephrase that. I know you know what's digging the holes and why. At least you have a pretty good idea. Spill it."

Pax and Storm exchange a look and Pax nods and says, "He might as well know, Storm. If this is what I think it is, we'll need allies, and it's not like it'll remain a secret for long anyway."

"Meet us in Pastor John's office tomorrow, Max. He'll explain it all, and we might learn something ourselves," Storm says. "Right now I need to get home, clean up and eat. You should, too. You've been working hard. Don't you have training with Sensei Hunter tonight?"

Max reluctantly agrees. I feel his frustration. I hate it when answers to my questions are delayed like that. It's even worse when no one will give me an answer at all. For once, I feel sympathy for the oaf.

~~~~~

As usual, we meet at the Fletchers after supper and train with Sensei Dylan in relative quiet. The strain of knowing and not knowing is beginning to take its toll. Sky doesn't come to the gym at all and I assume she's resting. I'd love to join her and take a nice long nap. After another night of interrupted sleep thanks to the earthquakes, I'm feeling very tired. And who knows if we'll have another quake tonight, all I know is that they seem to be getting stronger.

TWENTY-TWO

SKY

The quake is more than a minor tremor. A sound as loud as the roar of a stadium full of fans wakes me up to rolling waves of motion. My stomach turns, sick at the unnatural movement. I pull the covers over my head and pray that it stops. God, keep my family safe. God, keep Jewel's house from falling off the cliff. Disjointed thoughts and prayers rattle as hard in my brain as the earth rattles our house. I feel Mom's terror. Dad and Pax send out protective vibes, waves of strength and comfort. I expect it from my courageous brother, but this is new from Dad. Does Pax get this gift from our father and not from the aliens?

When it stops, I jump out of bed and run to Mom and Dad's room. Mom passes me in the hall. "Get outside, Sky," she yells, and turns the corner toward the kitchen. I know she's going to check her instruments.

Dad and Pax have put on boots and jackets, and Pax hurries me back to my room to do the same. I pull on a hoodie over my pajama top and slip my feet into sneakers without bothering to tie them.

It's cold outside, typical for a mid-September night. I'm glad Pax made me take the time to cover up. We sit in Dad's car with the heater going and wait for Mom. Her face is pale in the headlights when she emerges from the house and climbs into the passenger seat.

"We'll have to wait here a while. There should be aftershocks after a quake of that magnitude."

"What did it register?" asks Dad.

"It was a 6.0, a strong one. We should be hearing about it in the news tomorrow. I pray there are no injuries and not too much damage. Our house and the Adams' home should be fine. The O'Connells should be alright, too. Their log home is as sturdy as they come. I'm concerned for our less fortunate friends and neighbors."

"Dad," Pax says. "We'll know for sure tomorrow if the aliens have anything to do with the quakes. If someone discovers a hole in the morning, we can be pretty certain they dug it and whatever technology they're using is causing the tremors."

"I know, son," Dad says, sounding tired. "I know."

We wait for another half hour, and when no aftershocks occur, we go back inside. It's after four a.m. and none of us has gotten much sleep this week. I was eager to return to school in the morning, but I'm not sure I'll want to after this. I lie down, fully expecting to say awake the rest of the night.

To my surprise, I wake up to the shriek of the alarm clock.

~~~~

Pax drives us to school. I miss my little car, but I'm grateful for a brother who's willing to drive me places. My leg is fine, my face shows no signs of bruising, and I feel surprisingly chipper after last night's quake. Even the pain of my bruised ribs is barely noticeable.

Pastor John calls my name in the hallway before I can get to class. He strides down the hall toward me, eyes crinkled with his usual smile. "Sky, do you have a few minutes? I need to see you in my office."

I follow him wondering what he could need. We walk in and I'm surprised but pleased to see Jewel and Storm there. I pass the headmaster's desk and move to where a couch and two chairs face a brick fireplace on the opposite side. Pax follows us in and takes a seat on the couch next to Storm. He makes space for me between them. Max comes in last and grabs a chair from in front of the desk. Max?

Pastor John leans forward, clasps his hands in his lap and says, "You boys have been working on a special project for me since the morning after the first quake hit our area. Jewel was with you yesterday, and some of you know more than others. It's time to get all of you on the same page.

"Four nights ago, on the same day as your accident, Sky, Blue Mountain was at the epicenter of a minor earthquake. It happened in the middle of the night and most people didn't feel it. Coral Fletcher, who keeps track of such things, says it was a magnitude 3.9. A slightly stronger quake, measuring 4.2, occurred the next night, around the same time. A magnitude 4.9 quake hit on the third night."

"It woke me up at 4:30 in the morning," Jewel tells us.

"I think we all felt that one," Pastor John continues. "And then last night, we were hit again, only this one registered at 6.0. They're getting stronger and more dangerous every night. I assumed, of course, that the artifact is becoming more unstable, but something else has made me question that assumption."

"Artifact?" Max, who'd been slouching in his chair, straightens up. This is something no one has told him about. The feeling he projects is not the curiosity of someone wanting to learn, but something more sinister. His eagerness revolts me. Pax watches my face and sends soothing waves my way.

Pastor John ignores his question and continues, "This morning I received a call from Sheriff Green. After checking his house for damage and finding none, Hunter Smith went outside to do his warm-up exercises in the back yard, just as he does every morning. When he stumbled on a crack that must have been caused by the tremor the night before, he followed it into the woods and found a hole about six feet in diameter. He dropped a lit flashlight into it and says it never hit bottom, at least as far as he can tell. They might have broken through this time, and we're afraid they may have found the artifact."

"Hold on a minute," Max interrupts. "What's all this talk about an artifact? Who might have found it and why do they want it? Are they the same things that attacked Storm two weeks ago?"

"Patience, Max," says Pastor John. "I'll get to all of that after we figure out what our next step is. I promise, after I dismiss these kids to class, I'll tell you everything."

I don't like the sound of that. Does he mean everything unedited, or edited? What does Max have to do with our task? Will he keep the secret, or will he tell Marla and his unruly buddies? I don't trust Max.

"I think it's time for us to speak with the Watchers again." I watch Max's face as I make the suggestion. I wonder if they'll meet with us if he's there, too.

Storm agrees. "They'll know if anyone or anything is threatening the artifact, and they can tell us what to do."

"I'll contact Sequoia. She communicates with them regularly and will tell us what they think. And now you four get to class. I'll fill Max in when you're gone." Pastor John dismisses us. Pax picks up on my worry, but this time there's no comfort from him. He's worried, too.

My brother says nothing as he walks me to my class but I sense his unease. "What are you thinking?" I know I'm prodding but he's used to it.

"Sky, you don't trust Max, either, do you? I wonder what Pastor John is doing?"

"I have a feeling he's giving him the benefit of the doubt. He's known him practically all his life, hasn't he? Maybe there's more to Max than we know."

"You would know better than anyone the kind of vibes he gives off. He and Marla are up to no good."

I have to agree with him, but Pastor John doesn't strike me as someone who can't read people. Pax is right. Our headmaster is up to something, too.

I finish my homework in our free period at the end of the day and head out to Pax's car as soon as the bell rings, but it isn't in the parking lot. I'll bet he's running another errand and forgot that he's my ride home.

"Sky!" I hear Jewel call and turn around. She's in the next row, holding the passenger door to her green SUV open.

"You're riding with me. Your mom invited me to stay for supper, and then we have training. Are you coming?"

As soon as I buckle in, I sense that she's disturbed about something. "What's bothering you?" I ask, and she doesn't seem a bit surprised that those are my first words to her since our meeting this morning.

"Other than nightly earthquakes, someone poking holes in the earth, alien attacks, Storm's injury and now yours, and the fact we can't seem to escape that we're expected to fix the world, you mean? Other than that, nothing's bothering me."

The absurdity strikes us at the same time, and we start laughing. Each time the laughter dies out, one of us says, "Other than…" and adds something new. By the time we get to my house, we're in tears from laughing so hard. I sense that we're close to hysteria, and one more "other than" might tip us over the edge.

TWENTY-THREE

We're still eating meals that were brought to us after my accident, or should I say incident. The industrial sized freezer in the basement is packed with them, and Mom figures she won't have to cook for at least a month. She adds a fresh salad to the reheated lasagna, and Jewel and I dig in.

Pax and Storm come home halfway through our meal, and Mom gets plates ready for them. They're too busy eating to talk, so we still know nothing about their errand. Judging by the discussion we had this morning with Pastor John, I assume it had to do with the hole in Hunter Smith's woods.

After supper, Storm cleans up with practiced ease, and we enjoy the spectacle of dishes floating through the air, dipping under the faucet that turned on all by itself, and neatly stacking themselves in the dishwasher. I secretly wish I had gotten his particular gift. Life would be so much easier.

It feels good to participate in training again. I help Jewel practice her forms and teach her the next one. Each form, or kata, builds upon the last, and it takes time to master them and earn new belts. Jewel is strong and quick, and Dad, rather Sensei, is pleased with her progress.

We take a water break and watch the boys spar. They've been trained in different forms of martial arts. I recognize my brother's offensive movements, but not Storm's lightning quick responses. He manages to turn the tables, and Pax is forced to defend himself. Sensei calls the match; the boys bow, grab their towels and take the bottles of water we hand them.

"I wouldn't normally do this," Sensei says, nodding his thanks to Jewel for the water she offers him. "Storm has picked up some interesting moves in mixed martial arts training. He's agreed to show us what we're not familiar with, and is willing to learn from us, as well. It's highly unusual to mix disciplines, but as he says," he gives a nod to Storm, "if his life or someone he cares about is threatened, all bets are off."

I'm thrilled to hear this. Dad has always been a stickler for the purity of Shotokan. This departure must mean he's impressed by Storm's moves, or maybe it's just that he's impressed with Storm. I tune my senses to Storm's and feel his satisfaction. I wonder if Jewel sees a difference in his aura.

~~~~~

We usually go our separate ways right after training, but Dad sits us down on the mats. He looks serious. "It's time that you kids stay close to each other when you're away from the safety of your home and school."

I feel Storm bristle at this. "With all due respect, Sensei," he says. "I'd rather be able to go my own way, as I've done for years now."

"Noted," Dad says. "However, you were attacked not once, but twice. You weren't alone either time, but those with you were unable to help you. By staying close, you'll learn how your gifts can be used to complement and enhance each other. You'll be watching out for each other, and protecting each other. It has nothing to do with any weakness on your part, or on the part of any of you.

"When Sky was attacked she was alone. Could her injuries have been prevented if one or more of you had been with her? We can't know, of course, but we want you to avoid being alone until all this is resolved."

"My bike doesn't have a back seat for a passenger," Storm objects. His excuse is lame and he knows it.

"Then you and your bike will ride alongside someone driving a car. It's not forever, Storm."

Jewel is chewing her bottom lip, and I feel impatience mixed with a little excitement coming from her. I resolve to ask her about it later.

Before we can talk, she says she needs to get home and Pax follows her in his car. Mom and I settle in to watch the news.

*****

Breaking News: "An outbreak of twisters destroyed homes and businesses from Texas to Tennessee last night. At least three were determined to be rare F5 tornadoes with winds topping three hundred miles per hour and leaving massive paths of destruction. The number of casualties is still unknown."

"Locally, residents of Blue Mountain, North Carolina, were shaken last night by a fourth earthquake in as many nights, this one measuring a magnitude 6.0 on the Richter scale. The tremors have residents concerned that another might hit tonight. Officials are urging people to be calm, and to seek safety outside if it happens again. There has been little damage reported." – Kyle Johnson reporting for Cherokee Nation News."

*****

Reports of insane weather events and natural disasters take up more and more of the news every day. I've even heard reports of UFO sightings and more strange sounds in the atmosphere aired on national news.

Jewel has been looking into how these events have increased in number and intensity over the last seventeen years, but the whole idea that our beautiful planet is sick disturbs me too much. If I could, I'd rather ignore it. Ignorance is bliss, they say.

I hug Mom and go to bed fully dressed so I'm not caught off guard if the ground moves again.

TWENTY-FOUR

There was no quake last night. I slept soundly, for once, which has me awake and ready to go when Pax and I leave early to meet Jewel at her house. I decide to ride along with her while my brother follows us in his car.

As soon as we buckle in and Jewel turns out onto the main road I find I can't hold my tongue any longer.

"Okay," I say in my most no-nonsense voice. "Give it up, Jewel. You have something on your mind and I want to know what it is."

"I can't keep any secrets from you, can I?" She pretends to pout, but I feel the excitement she's trying to suppress. She checks her mirror and I know she sees Pax behind us. I sense her interest in him.

"Nope," I say. "So spill it."

"First promise you won't tell the boys just yet." I promise, but mentally cross my fingers. It will depend on what she says. She continues, "See this wristband?" She holds out her arm with the fitness monitor. Naturally, I've noticed it, and I've wondered why she taps it so often. I had thought it must be a nervous habit.

"What about it?" I ask.

"It's one of Dad's inventions. My parents and I each have one, and it allows us to speak to each other telepathically."

"Do you mean like the Watchers? How is that possible?" I think about having my parents in my head all the time and add, "Aren't you invading each other's privacy?"

"No, Silly. That would be awful. We call each other using a code. If someone isn't available, they tap that they're busy. We have to answer every call in order to let the caller know we aren't unconscious or worse, even if it's to decline."

"What if you're sleeping?"

"It's also a fitness monitor and registers when you sleep. It sounds complicated, but it's really easy to use."

"So, is your Dad marketing this? He could be a bazillionaire with an invention like this."

"He won't. Imagine if the wrong people get hold of it. With some modifications they could use it for spying or, even worse, mind control. It has to be kept a closely guarded secret." Jewel spins it around on her wrist. It looks loose.

"Why are you telling me about it?" I feel her excitement rise and it worries me.

"He's talked to your parents and Storm's family, and they've agreed that he should develop one for each of you, too." So that's what she's excited about. I feel a little uneasy. Do I want my family to have access to my thoughts?

"How do you keep them from reading your thoughts?"

"They only hear what you think to them, like speech. When you're done talking, you press on the face of the wristband and end the conversation. It's just the same as if you were talking normally."

I grow silent as I think about the significance of having mental conversations with my parents. What if I forget to end the conversation and they overhear thoughts I don't want to share? I'm not so sure this is a good idea until Jewel says, "We four will be able to talk to each other, too. We wouldn't have to stay as close physically if we can instantly call for help when we need it. Storm should like that idea."

It's sounding better. Considering the recent attacks, the earthquakes and those mysterious holes, I can see where this might come in handy in an emergency.

"When will your Dad have them available?"

"That's the thing, Sky. The interface is really complex, and it'll take time for him to tie all the threads together. Morse code is what we use now, but that won't work in our connection to each other. We need something that will link us instantly, and he's working on developing that code, too."

Jewel is still excited, but the tension of having to keep it all to herself has eased. She's given it to me, instead.

"When are you planning to tell the boys?"

"When we know for sure that it'll work. Why get their hopes up if it can't happen? I shouldn't have told you, either, but you have a way of drawing me out."

"Yeah," I say. "I wish I hadn't pressured you into telling me. What makes you think I can keep a secret from my brother? He'll sense it."

We park next to Pax's SUV and Storm pulls up in a black, slightly dented pickup.

I get out and ask through his open window, "New truck?"

"New for me," he answers. He opens the door and hops out, trying not to look pleased. I feel his pleasure, though. He doesn't fool me at all.

"It beats riding a motorcycle in the winter," Pax observes. He walks around the truck, admiring it and commenting on the tires and rims; boys and their toys.

Jewel and I turn away and head toward the school. Max and his Lost Boys crow and strut by the front door. It's like watching a twisted version of Peter Pan. Marla leans against the wall with her arms crossed and her narrowed eyes staring at us. Doesn't she ever blink? She makes my skin crawl.

TWENTY-FIVE

PAX

"Nice truck. It's funny you didn't mention it yesterday when Dad suggested we stay close." I'd already known about the truck, of course, but I didn't want to call him out on it in front of the group. "You don't have an extra seat on your dirt bike. That's rich."

He throws a light punch at my arm. "Yeah, thanks for not saying anything. It didn't work, anyway."

Storm and I skipped last period yesterday to meet Wolf at the car lot. He helped Storm pick out the truck, opting for strength and the quality of the engine rather than beauty. I dropped my scent guard and sniffed for rust or leaks and was surprised to find none. It has dents, but in my opinion, they give it character. There's no point in buying a brand new work truck unless you have a business that demands it. This pickup will come in handy when we explore the latest borehole in Hunter Smith's woods.

It seems that the aliens used some kind of laser to cut the circular holes in the ground, given the smooth sides. The question is, which of the two races did it? My bets are on the Dracans. Wouldn't the Allarans already know where the artifacts are?

After Storm and Wolf purchased the truck, we swung by Mr. Smith's place. By the time we got there it was too dark to set up any safety measures.

If this is deeper than the others, as Mr. Smith seems to think, we'll need a heavy duty winch, longer cables, and who knows what else. Max can get the equipment with his dad's help, and Storm's truck can be used to anchor the winch and cable. We should be able to get to it this afternoon.

We get to class just as the last bell rings.

Jewel's head is bent over an open book on her desk and she doesn't look up as I brush past her. The location of my desk, behind hers and a few seats over, gives me a great vantage point where I can admire her without giving away my intense interest. Am I the only one who notices how her hair appears black until light hits it? Even the artificial light in the room brings out rainbows. I wonder how it would look to her if she could see it with her enhanced ability. I let down my guard, locate her scent and breathe deeply. She smells wonderful, but the odor of the other bodies in the room just about knocks me out— big mistake. I turn to listen to the teacher, but I'm fully aware of Jewel the entire time.

Once again, Pastor John calls Storm, Max, and me into his office, excusing us from the remainder of our classes for the day. I'm still wondering why Max is being included in our investigations.

The three of us squeeze into the cab of Storm's truck. He doesn't have an extended cab like Sequoia's, but it's wide enough if you don't mind crowding. I thank God for my scent guard when I get a whiff of Max's odor. I'm in the middle and for some reason, perhaps hygiene related, Storm's scent isn't offensive to me, but Max is another story.

"Mind opening the windows, guys?" Thankfully, they both comply and the fresh air is lifesaving.

Storm glances across me at Max. His face is tense. "So, Max, what did Pastor John tell you about the artifacts?"

Max straightens up from his customary slouch. "Artifacts? You mean there's more than one?"

I may have to reevaluate his intelligence level. He might be brighter than he looks. He certainly caught that little slip of Storm's.

"What did he say, Max?" I attempt to deflect where this is going. "What do you think the artifact is?"

He gives me a disgusted look and says, "You know. It's an old pyramid someone buried a long time ago, right? For some reason the things that attacked Storm want it and we have to keep them from getting it."

"Yeah, that's right," Storm looks relieved. As I suspected, Pastor John gave him enough of the story to garner his help and keep him from interfering with us without revealing what it does and what role we may have to play. I have a feeling that Max is in on this only because his dad is the Sheriff. It's strange that Sheriff Green, who knows all about the artifacts, has kept his son in the dark all this time.

We arrive at Hunter Smith's house and drive the truck around back. The hole isn't too far into the woods and with some maneuvering; Storm is able to back the truck close enough to it. He sets wooden chocks behind all four wheels while Max and I set up the winch and attach one end of the cable to it. We put on the climbing gear the sheriff provided for us, including miner's caps and webbed belts with extra flashlights, batteries, and water. Storm straps a leather sheath to his leg and examines the blade of his hunting knife before he slides it in. Max drops the unattached end of the cable into the hole and it uncoils until it reaches bottom.

"Looks to be about seventy feet, more or less," he says, and winches the cable back up.

Storm steps to the edge. "I'll go in first and float you down."

"Who's going to man the winch?" Max asks, clearly unwilling to stay behind.

"We won't need it as long as I'm around and no one else is nearby. We'll be fine. Let's go see where the hole ends up, and whether it leads to another tunnel." He disappears down the shaft.

Max is annoyed. "Then what the heck do we need a winch for?"

"Who's next?" Storm's voice echoes as if from a great distance.

"Thanks, but I'll use the cable," Max puts on the safety harness. "Ready. Lower me away, Pax."

Max steps to the edge and I start the winch. It's slow, but he finally reaches bottom. I leave the cable at the bottom and follow as soon as the coast is clear and Storm is ready for me. The drop is quick and smooth. I lower my scent guard on the way down and smell scorched earth and something metallic that I can't identify. I'm surprised at the easy landing and quickly put the guard back up knowing I won't be able to smell anything besides Max.

The bottom of the borehole slopes downward and leads into a tunnel. We turn on our headlamps and find Mr. Smith's flashlight several feet in. From the top it must have looked like it disappeared into a bottomless pit. The tunnel is tall enough to stand in, but not wide enough for more than one person to walk at a time. Storm takes the lead, Max falls in behind him, and I take up the rear. I feel better knowing that we have close tabs on Max.

I sense he's getting increasingly agitated; he probably needs something to keep his mind off the dark tunnel. "How long have you and Marla been dating?"

"What do you care?" he snaps.

"Sorry," I try to keep my voice steady so he doesn't hear how annoyed I am. "It looks like we'll be working together, and I thought we could get to know each other a little better."

"Why? Do you have your eye on her?"

I have to bite my tongue to keep from snapping at the moron. "Forget it. I think I prefer the silence anyway."

We plod on and I lose track of time and distance. Storm stops suddenly.

"Hold up," he whispers. "I hear something."

I hold my breath and strain my ears and after a moment, I hear the echo of distant voices. "Lights off," he orders.

"No way," Max says aloud, and I jab him in the ribs.

"Shut up and turn your lamp off," I whisper, "Unless you want the aliens to catch you down here."

The darkness is complete. I have to give Max some credit. He keeps his whimpers quiet.

TWENTY-SIX

Storm moves forward with shuffling steps. Max holds on to his belt, while I grab Max's. It's unlikely that we'll be separated in these close quarters, but it's reassuring to have some human contact. We round a curve and see light ahead. Storm crouches and motions for us to do the same. He unsheathes his knife and holds it lightly in his right hand. I don't blame him. If I had a weapon, I'd hold it ready, too.

We inch toward the opening where the light is coming from, but a boulder partially blocks our view. The little we can see seems to be the edge of a cave. The voices speak again and the way they echo means the chamber must be a good-sized cavern.

"How much farther?" a woman asks.

Max tugs on my arm at the sound of the female voice. In the glow his face looks pasty. I motion for him to stay silent.

A deep, guttural voice answers in strangely-accented English, "Soon, woman. We blast and continue. You are welcome to leave and return to the surface if this is too much for you."

"Alone?" she sounds frightened.

"Of course," the male answers. "We will continue until we find it or cannot proceed further."

At that, he says something in a language I don't recognize and a loud buzzing causes us to cover our ears. I smell burning rock and feel a blast of heat. I hope the woman has some protective covering on. The heat is intense for a few seconds even in our sheltered location.

Storm signals to me to retreat, and I gladly head back into the tunnel. We turn our headlamps back on and move at a brisk pace. No one says a word, and soon we're at the base of the pit.

He tells Max, "There's no time for the winch. Hold on to the cable as I lift you. It will give you some stability until you're topside." Max nods and does what he's been instructed to do. He gives us a thumbs-up as soon as he clears the hole. I ascend next, and it's like being in a floorless elevator.

As soon as Storm's head clears the hole, Max blurts out, "I know that woman!"

"Tell us on the way home," Storm says as he turns on the winch to raise the cable. I pile the climbing gear and our headlamps into the truck bed and Max clears the chocks and throws them in. We work quickly. There's no telling if the woman followed us out or stayed with the diggers. We aren't willing to chance being discovered.

We all breathe a sigh of relief when we clear Hunter Smith's property and turn on the main road. That's when it dawns on me that we never got a look at who was digging the tunnel. Were they Allarans or Dracans?

"Spill it, Max," Storm says.

"That woman is Marla's mother," he says.

"Oh, man," I reach across Max and roll down the window. No sense in suffocating. "We'd better report it to Pastor John and our folks right away."

"I don't understand," Max stares out the window and seems to have lost his bravado. "What does Mrs. Snow have to do with all this?"

TWENTY-SEVEN

We get back to school in time for last period and go straight to the Headmaster's office. When Pastor John calls for us to enter, I'm surprised to see Jewel and Sky already there, sitting close together on the couch. Sky's eyes are red, as if she's been crying. I rush over to her and pull her close.

"What is it, Sky?"

"It's you, you big oaf," she shouts. "You and Storm, getting yourselves into trouble without us. How could you?"

Her gift must be getting stronger if she sensed our adventure in the tunnel. I don't recall being afraid, and no one was hurt, so what, exactly, did she sense? I send calm to her until I feel her relax and ask her. "What did you feel, Sky?"

As she tells me, I notice that Jewel's eyes are red, too, and my heart twists into a knotty lump.

"I didn't realize that you're a constant presence in my mind until today, Pax; and not just you. One moment you were there, and the next you weren't. You stopped. I searched and searched for you and felt nothing but a void. Then I searched for Storm.

"Do you remember the day you were attacked, Storm? You were so far away, and yet I felt it. I felt your rage and the pain when the aliens seared your leg. Since then, I feel you as much as Pax, and today, you were gone, too."

She breaks down in sobs and I hug her tightly. Jewel hands her a tissue and glares at me. I wish I knew why. Why did my sister stop feeling my presence? Was it something in the tunnel?

Pastor John says in a soothing voice, "I told the girls where you'd gone, and when Sky said she'd lost you, I reminded her that you were in an alien-made hole and there might be something in it that's blocking her senses. I'm afraid it didn't help much."

Max stands apart near the window and listens intently. He knew about Storm's gift, but this may be the first time he's hearing about Sky's.

"Who are you people?" he asks in a shaky voice.

Pastor John goes to stand in front of Max and grabs both his shoulders. "If I tell you, Max, you have to keep it in strictest confidence. Do you understand? You won't be able to tell anyone, not even Marla."

"Don't worry about that," Max replies. "I just found out her mother is working with the aliens that dug the holes."

"What!?" Jewel exclaims. Pastor John sits back down and Sky gives Jewel an 'I told you so' kind of look.

Storm tells them about the tunnel and how we heard voices. "One of them was hers. Max recognized her right away. Pastor, what do you think she was doing with them?"

"Jewel," Pastor John says instead, "tell Max what you see when the glasses are off."

She takes her glasses off and I melt at the brilliant turquoise of her eyes. Max gapes, his mouth hanging open.

"I see auras, Max. They're energy fields that show up as bright light in animals and as colors around humans. Yours is brown with streaks of muddy red."

"What does that mean?" he asks. "What do the colors mean?"

"I'm not sure," Jewel continues. "All I know is that every human has a distinct aura. Years ago my mom and I encountered an alien in the park. Mom only saw its disguise as an older woman, but I see through disguises. It had scaly skin, a longish snout and lots of very sharp teeth. The thing had a glow, like animals do, but no aura. When I looked at Marla without my glasses, she had an aura, but it was very faint. I also saw through her disguise."

"Meaning?" Max is growing impatient, and I see his face begin to twist in anger.

"Meaning she's only partly human."

Max's fist hits the wall with a resounding boom and Storm jumps to his feet and immobilizes him without touching him. Max's face turns bright red and his eyes bulge with rage. The headmaster opens a mini-refrigerator next to his desk and pulls out a bottle of water.

"Calm down, Max. Have some water. This isn't helping anything."

I feel waves of peace coming off Sky, and Max soon relaxes.

"Sorry," he finally says. "I can't believe my girlfriend isn't human. What is she then? An alien? I'm dating an alien?" He takes a deep breath and says, "You can let me go, Storm. I'm over it."

He shakes out his arms, looks at each one of us and says, "If she's an alien, then what are you?"

No one answers him.

"The question is," I start, "what blocked Sky's access to us, and does it block our abilities? I dropped my scent guard on the way down the shaft and noticed an unfamiliar metallic scent. At the bottom, I put it up again and had no reason to use it in the tunnel. Storm, did you use your telekinesis?"

"Not until we were out of the tunnel," Storm shakes his head. "It makes sense that they'd have a way to block us. Maybe that's why everything I threw at them bounced off the day they attacked me."

"This complicates matters." Pastor John paces in front of the windows. He frowns and massages his temples. I don't doubt that we give him a major headache.

Max speaks up as if he's just now processed what I'd said. "Wait, what's a scent guard?"

Storm laughs, "It's to keep him from smelling you. You are pretty ripe."

Max stomps and throws his arms out to the side in an aggressive gesture, but doesn't move any closer. No one wants a repeat performance of his lack of control.

"What happened today, Sky, when you lost us?" My sister is calm again, but Jewel seems a little on edge. She answers for Sky.

"It happened in Advanced Biology, after lunch. Mr. Abrams was talking about doing a section on Cryptozoology when Sky stood up and a wave of shock and fear came off her, causing pandemonium in the room. Some kids fell to the floor and covered their heads while others rushed for the door. Mr. Abrams hid behind his desk. I didn't know what to do so I grabbed Sky's hand and pulled her to the headmaster's office. Her fear and grief affected everyone in the school. We saw kids weeping in the hallway as they scrambled to leave the building. She's more effective than a fire alarm."

"I feel terrible about it," Sky looks at Pastor John and I'm sure he sees, or feels, how contrite she is. "I honestly could not control it. I panicked."

"It's over now," he says. "Everyone calmed down as soon as you sensed the boys again, probably when they exited the tunnel. Now that you know about the blocking, you'll have no reason to panic the next time."

"Next time?" Max exclaims. "I'm not going back in there. What are we supposed to do there anyway? Fight those things? With what?"

The same questions have been running through my mind. Exactly what are we doing? Will we find the artifact by following them, and if that's the case, won't they find it first? How can we fight them or, bigger question, how can we fix the artifact if our gifts are blocked? Aren't the Watchers supposed to lead us to it, and are they prepared to keep it safe from the Dracans? Now my head is aching.

"I think we've all had enough for one day." The headmaster stands from his desk and opens the office door. "You kids go home and we'll figure things out when we've all had something to eat and a good rest."

How are we supposed to rest if we can't get any answers?

TWENTY-EIGHT

STORM

I really want to take my bike out for a fast ride in the woods, but it'll have to wait until Saturday. I'm grateful for the truck, but riding clears my head and makes me feel alive. I want to kill the aliens and be done with it, but it's apparently not that easy. What do they want with us, anyway?

This line of thinking gets me nowhere, so I switch gears and think about Sky. She senses everyone's feelings and projects her emotions to them. I can see how projecting would be a defense mechanism. How horrible it would be if all she could do was feel the emotions of everyone around her. That would be enough to drive anyone insane. She said she senses me. Is it different from the waves of input she gets from everyone else? I know she and Pax have a special connection. Is she saying she shares that kind of connection with me?

If what I feel for her is coming from her, then is it real? Are the feelings mine or hers? Or both? I hope it is coming from her because I don't need any romantic complications in my life right now. I have to focus on my goal, which is to kill my enemies and find and fix the artifacts. I can't allow Sky to distract me.

The cabin is quiet when I arrive. I check all the rooms, but Sequoia and Wolf must be out. I walk outside and see both their vehicles parked behind the shed. Maybe they're in the woods, or they went for a walk. I try to shove the uneasy feeling aside. They're fine, I tell myself.

I heat up some leftovers. Sequoia is a fine cook and the food tastes even better this time around. After supper, I clean up and leave a note on the counter to let them know that I've gone to train with the others.

Dylan answers the door and ushers me inside. "Is Wolf at home?' he asks. "I've been calling him, but he isn't answering his phone."

"He might not have it on him," I answer. Usually I'm the one who forgets about the phone. It irritates me no end to see kids with their eyes glued to the electronics in their hands, ignoring the world around them. Come to think of it, I've never seen Jewel, Pax, or Sky with phones, either. The problem is, I can't remember ever seeing Wolf without his phone clipped to his belt. He does always have it, as far as I know. An uncomfortable premonition sneaks up on me. Something is wrong.

"Both Wolf and Sequoia were gone when I got home. I saw their trucks parked at the house, but I figured they went into the woods on foot. It isn't unusual. The fact that they didn't leave me a note is out of the ordinary."

Dylan pulls out his cellphone. "I'll try Sequoia's phone. You go on down and get ready to spar with Pax, and I'll be right there."

"If you don't mind, I'll wait and see if you connect with her."

Dylan nods and dials. He waits, hangs up and dials again. When he begins to speak I turn to leave. She must have answered and all is well. I stop when I hear Dylan say, "Call me when you get this message."

"Wait here," he says and heads downstairs. I wait for what seems like an hour but might have been only a few minutes until he returns. "They're changing. We're going back to your place."

Pax and the girls crowd into the hall with me and I notice anxiety in Sky's face for a moment. Then she composes herself and I feel a wave of peace. This time it doesn't help.

The girls pile into Pax's SUV while Dylan climbs into my truck and we go back to the cabin. It looks deserted, like the life has gone out of it. I remind myself they were here just this morning. Nobody has deserted anything. I hadn't left a light on when I left earlier, and that's why it looks so eerie. Sequoia always leaves the porch light burning and a lamp on in the living room until we're all at home, even if I come home after they've gone to bed.

Dylan goes in first and turns on the porch and hall lights. We go from room to room to see if anything is out of place, but Dylan tells us to be sure we don't touch anything. Pax walks over to a coat-rack where Wolf and Sequoia's jackets hang and sniffs it.

"I'll track them, Storm." He walks out to the porch and scents the air. "They were out here no more than four or five hours ago." We follow him into the yard, where he stops and turns in circles.

"Why'd you stop?" Sky asks.

"This is where the trail ends," he says. "Right here, like they just disappeared."

Jewel looks at the sky. "The Sentinels are up there. Do you think one of them took them?"

"Either the Allarans or the Dracans," Dylan says. "At this point, I'm not sure which is worse."

He calls Sheriff Green, who shows up a half hour later with two of his deputies. I'm grateful they didn't use sirens and flashing lights. My aching soul wants dark and quiet. Has Sky's gift rubbed off on me? I understand now what she meant when she said she didn't feel Pax and me. I don't feel the constant, calming presence of my aunt and uncle, and the emptiness is desolate.

Dylan invites me to spend the night at their house, and I'm happy to have the company. I grab my phone and charger in case they return and call me. If the Allarans have my folks, they could drop them off at any time, like they did with Mom. I pray to the God I'm not on speaking terms with that they aren't with the Dracans. If they are, I may never see them again.

The twins and I watch the news after their parents go to their room. None of it is good, but it keeps my mind occupied.

*****

Breaking News: "An unseasonal snowstorm swept in from the Great Lakes and dumped twelve inches of snow as far south as

Philadelphia this morning. The governor of Pennsylvania has called for a state of emergency and asks folks to stay indoors and off the roads."

"In other news, another rift in the earth opened up in Abilene, Texas, tearing through a crowded parking lot and breaking across two main roads. At least fifty parked cars fell into the hole, but, thankfully, no injuries were reported. Local businesses have been evacuated."

"Tonight, winter weather and wind alerts stretch all the way from California to Indiana. Damaging winds and tornadoes are expected all along the front." – Kyle Johnson reporting for Cherokee Nation News."

*****

"It's getting worse," Pax observes. "A day doesn't go by without terrible storms, earthquakes, tornadoes, or hurricanes. How long do you think it'll be before the Watchers call us to fix that artifact?"

"What are they waiting for?" Sky wonders aloud. "And where are Wolf and Sequoia?"

The guest bedroom has its own bathroom. Sky's question echoes endlessly in my brain as I shower and brush my teeth. It doesn't take me long to fall asleep on the comfortable bed, but the last thought I recall is 'Where are they?'

TWENTY-NINE

I'm up before dawn and hurry to get dressed. The cellphone is fully charged on the nightstand, so I disconnect it from the charger and put it in my pocket. It feels odd to carry it, but what if Wolf or Sequoia calls? I can't risk missing it.

Coral Fletcher is already in the kitchen preparing breakfast. "Good morning, Storm. I thought you'd want to get home early and check on your folks, but you're not leaving without eating." She sets a plate of scrambled eggs and sausage on the counter, pours coffee, and sits across from me. Her eyes are nearly as blue as her daughter's and shine with a kindness that wells up from a loving heart.

I hesitate to ask, but her face invites candor. "Coral, what do you remember from your abduction?"

She isn't surprised by the question. "I don't recall much, Storm. They did a pretty good job of wiping our memories, but flashes do come back to me now and then." She sips her coffee and the expression in her eyes grows distant.

"There were two of them in the room where I lay on what felt like an operating table. Tall, shiny silver skin, white hair, big eyes; they didn't speak. A lamp over the table shone a bright light on me but didn't hurt my eyes. I thought that was odd. Isn't it irrational that nothing else felt strange to me? I don't recall feeling any pain or fear.

"When we woke up at our camp, we didn't know I'd been taken. Our guide Anik remembered everything, but didn't share that information with us until much later. Other than his being abnormally quiet, there was no indication that anything unusual had happened. I felt a little sick and dizzy, but attributed it to the pregnancy, which I found out about at the doctor's later that day."

"Thanks, Coral. I just hope the Allarans took my folks rather than the reptilian creatures that killed my parents."

"I'm so sorry, Storm. This must be terrible for you. Please stay with us until they're found."

I appreciate her offer and will probably take her up on it, but for now, I have to get back to the cabin in case they've returned. I quickly finish my breakfast and treat her to my dish-clearing skills. She gives me a quick hug and sends me on my way.

The sun is rising over the mountains as I drive the winding road to the cabin. Morning mist covers the valley like a soft blue blanket, leaving mountaintops gleaming in the orange rays of the sun. When the Cherokee arrived in the area over a thousand years ago, they called the mountains the 'Land of the Blue Smoke,' and that's exactly what the morning fog looks like. It swirls and rises as the day heats up.

We'd left the porch light on last night. I go inside and turn it off. There's no life in the house. I collect a few clothes in a duffle bag and throw it in the truck for tomorrow. If Wolf and Sequoia don't return today, I'll stay at the Fletchers' again. Meanwhile, I plan to skip school and find some answers.

This time I take the road to the stomping grounds and park the truck outside of the gathering place. The equipment we used yesterday is still in the back, and I take one of the miner's caps and webbed belts with flashlight, extra batteries, canteen and rope. I strap on my hunting knife and head to the cave. I have no plan other than to contact the Watchers somehow and ask what, if anything, they know of my family's disappearance. Maybe they can help.

My cellphone ring startles me. When I answer, Sky is hysterical on the other line.

"Why did you run off?" she yells. "You should have woken us up!"

Pax must have grabbed the phone from her. His voice is much calmer. "Where are you, Storm?"

I left without waking them because I didn't want them to feel obligated to come with me. I'm used to doing everything on my own, but frankly, it's good to hear from them. I don't relish going into the cave alone. I tell him where I am and assure him I'll wait until they get here. After we hang up, it dawns on me that they'll be skipping school too.

It's no surprise to see Jewel with them when they drive up in Pax's car. I had a feeling Sky would contact her as soon as she found me. Sky and Pax get out and come to the truck. Jewel drags a heavy-looking backpack out of the backseat.

"What do you have in there," I ask her. "Rocks?"

"I brought water and snacks, Storm, or maybe you didn't plan to eat or drink anything during your spelunking adventure?" She sounds annoyed, and I don't blame her. It's still early in the morning.

Pax and I decide the girls should each have a miner's cap, and he would carry an extra flashlight. I grab my backpack, empty the schoolbooks out of it, and we divide the load from Jewel's between us. I take the lead along the trail to the cave entrance.

"How do you propose we contact the Watchers?" Jewel snaps, clearly not in a good mood.

"You've had practice communicating telepathically with your parents," Sky says, and then she makes a choking sound. "Oh, sorry, Jewel. I didn't mean to say that out loud."

Pax and I stop in our tracks. "What are you talking about?" he asks. "Is that an ability we don't know about?"

She glares at Sky and then turns to us. "I didn't want to tell you until I knew for sure that Dad can do it."

"Do what?" I'm confused. What does her dad have to do with her ability to communicate mentally? She taps on her wristband and turns away from us. She's silent for a few long minutes.

Pax looks at me, shrugs and asks "What are you doing, Jewel?"

"I just talked with Dad, if you must know. He's making progress and thinks the bands will be ready to test in a couple of days." Now she's lost me. Bands? Then she presses on the face of her fitness monitor and I get it. That's how they connect, through wristbands.

"What, exactly, is he developing?" Pax hasn't figured it out yet.

"These," she says, holding up her wrist and pointing to the fitness monitor. "He's developing one for each of us so we can link to each other telepathically. We'll also be able to connect with our parents, and with your aunt and uncle, Storm."

"Do you mean we'll be able to read each other's minds?" I ask, hoping it isn't so. She explains how they work and it seems like a great idea, as long as we can maintain our privacy.

"It's too bad we don't already have them," the thought saddens me. "We'd know if Wolf and Sequoia are safe."

Jewel smacks Sky on the shoulder. "I wish you hadn't said anything."

"Me, too," Sky says. "Sorry. I wish I could take it back."

We start walking again and I ask, "Do you think your telepathic conversations with your parents will help you call the Watchers?"

"Maybe," she answers. "I can at least try."

When we get to the clearing in front of the entrance, Pax gingerly walks toward it with his hand out. I remember how we bounced off an invisible wall the last time the Watchers retreated into the cave. He assures us the barrier is no longer there. I take the lead again and we turn our headlamps and flashlights on and go in one at a time. Once inside, we gather in the large chamber where the others gawk at the massive stalactites and stalagmites decorating the cavern.

"We're going to the crystal grotto," I tell them. "We'll have to go single file and you'll need to walk carefully. It twists and dips in places, but the passage isn't long. Once we're in the larger cavern, Jewel, you try to link with the Watchers."

She nods and I look for the broken stalagmite. The entrance is there in the ground and I drop in. I float Sky down behind me and feel her pleasure at the sensation of flying for a brief moment. I want to take her outside and let her soar over the treetops, but for now, I have to concentrate on getting Jewel and then Pax safely to the underground passage.

The last time I came this way, I stopped at the entrance to the cavern and turned back. This time, we carefully make our way to the center of the grotto.

"It's magical," breathes Sky. Waves of wonder come off her and make my heart speed up. I feel the magic, but it's hers, not the grotto's. I have a strong urge to gather her in my arms and kiss her. Pax breaks the spell.

"Impressive," he says. "Was this a quartz mine at one time?" He goes to a wall and examines it. "May I borrow your knife, Storm?" he asks and reaches toward me.

That's when the buzzing in my head starts and I hear, *Star Child, do not remove any part of this cavern.* Pax and I freeze with my knife suspended between us. I call it back to its sheath.

"I guess I didn't need telepathy after all," Jewel whispers.

Three small figures seem to float through an opening at the far side of the cavern. It becomes clear that they know what we're here for when one of them says, *Sequoia and her mate have been taken by the Dracans.*

My heart drops and I have a sick feeling in my stomach. Have I lost them, too? "Where?" I manage to choke out.

They have them in one of their underground bases, far from here.

I can't speak, so Pax asks, "Why did they take them? What do they want?"

We believe they want to draw the four of you away from the artifact.

Pax points out, "They're digging for the artifact right now. If the three of you are here, who is protecting it?"

My head throbs. Pax and Jewel are rubbing their temples and Sky has her hands pressed to the top of her skull. Their mind-speak is getting to all of us. Does Jewel experience this buzzing when she and her parents speak this way?

We are four. I'm not surprised. There are four of them, four of us, four Sentinels and four sides to a tetrahedron. Four is a significant number in the Cherokee culture, too, and I wonder exactly what the number signifies to the aliens.

Pax continues, "How close are they to finding it?"

111

Not close. It is deeper than they know. Creator hid it well. However, the time rapidly approaches when you will be summoned to its aid. Until then, we will protect it.

"How can we rescue Sequoia and Wolf?" Sky asks the question that's been burning inside me. How can we find them, much less get them away from those monsters?

We have told you that you will have help. It is time that you meet the ones you, Jewel, rightly call the Sentinels. They have the answers you seek.

They turn to leave and Pax says, "Wait, why don't you want us to take anything from this cave? It's just quartz."

It is more than quartz. The artifact needs minerals and crystals for sustenance. The crystals in this cavern provide energy. As long as they are not disturbed, they are helping to keep the artifact from deteriorating more rapidly. You need the time, young Star Children.

At that, they leave the grotto.

"Let's get out of here," I lead the way back and we're soon in the main cavern.

"We need a drink," Sky and Jewel say at the same time. They look at each other and giggle. I think their brains must feel as fried as mine. The cave is cool and dry and we find a place to sit on the floor where we can remain close together. It feels good to take the heavy backpack off.

Jewel rummages in the pack and hands out granola bars and water. We're each caught up in our own thoughts and no one speaks until I say it's time to go. We gather our things and make our way to the narrow entrance.

"Hold up," I see a shadow over the opening. Déjà vu. "We have company." I mentally prepare myself for a fight with another Dracan ship. Pax moves close to me and the girls line up behind us. I take the first step outside.

THIRTY

JEWEL

I crouch behind Storm as he approaches the cave entrance. Rocks lift into the air on both sides of us. I hear Pax sniffing. He grabs Storm's shirt and pulls him back.

"It's not them," he whispers. "Someone is out there waiting, but it isn't a Dracan."

"All I saw the last time was the ship," Storm retorts. "Can you scent the difference between a Dracan and Allaran ship?"

"There might not be a ship out there," Pax replies. "We can't see anything from here. I smell something alive and I don't recognize the scent, but it's much more bearable than Dracan stink."

"Okay. I won't throw anything until I get a visual. Fair enough?"

Pax nods and follows Storm to the opening with Sky and me trailing close behind.

"It's a Sentinel," I call out as soon as I see the craft floating just above the treetops. Storm and Pax glance up and then at each other and shake their heads.

Sky takes a longer look and says, "Sorry, Jewel. Can't see it. Are you sure you're not imagining things?" She's teasing, of course. I know she believes me.

"It's there, but more importantly, so is he," I nod toward a tall person standing by the trees at the edge of the clearing. He's dressed in shiny metallic-looking coveralls, similar to the clothing the Watchers wear, but this is no little bald guy. He towers over the boys. His skin throws off prisms where sunlight hits it, and blends in various shades of electric blue in shadow. Long, loose hair, so white it reflects the colors of the woods, blows in the wind. His eyes, the same size and shape as ours, glow in swirls of colors I cannot name. He has no aura, but his entire form is encased in a soft light. His beauty stuns me. The creature smiles and reveals two rows of perfectly pearlescent teeth.

Waves of joy come from Sky and I feel her exultation. Perhaps she's reflecting mine back to me. I steal a glance at the boys. Pax is frowning so deeply his eyebrows meet over his wrinkled nose. Storm scowls and I hear a low growl coming from his throat.

"Who are you?" Storm asks, "Do you know what happened to Sequoia and Wolf?"

"I am Vega. It is good to see you, Storm." His deep voice feels like silk running over my skin. I see Storm wince. Does he hear it differently? Pax hasn't lost his frown, only now he's looking at me.

Storm answers with a question, "How do you know my name?" He closes his hands into fists and relaxes his elbows. I can tell he's ready to fight by his stance—legs apart and knees slightly bent. Pax stands at the ready as well. What's up with these guys? Can't they tell Vega is our friend?

"I have no wish to fight you, Storm." Vega's voice soothes like chocolate and I'm a marshmallow melting between two graham crackers. What is wrong with me? Maybe the boys are right to be cautious. By her drooling smile and the vague look on her face, I guess that Sky is as mesmerized as I am.

"Of course you wouldn't know who I am. Please forgive me and allow me to introduce myself properly. I am Vega, the scientist whose DNA you share, Storm. I have watched you grow to a strong young warrior."

"You abducted my mother?" Storm shouts. Twigs, leaves, rocks and loose soil begin twirling like a tiny whirlwind in front of Vega. I want to throw myself between him and Storm, but Sky grabs my arm as she senses my impulse.

Vega's voice changes as he says something unintelligible and the whirling mess drops to the ground. He maintains the tone and addresses Pax and Storm, "I understand your aggression, but it is better directed at those who killed your parents and now hold your aunt and uncle."

Both boys stand back and I watch the tension leave their faces and bodies. Apparently, Vega has a gift of his own; one voice for them, another for us.

I notice Vega's skin no longer sparkles. Clouds have obscured the sun and the wind is growing stronger. I look up at dark, angry clouds scudding across the sky.

"It's going to storm." Everyone is so focused on Vega I don't think they hear me. It doesn't matter. We all jump at the giant crack of lightning that hits too close.

"To the cave," Storm shouts and we scramble toward the entrance. The first drops of rain fall, followed quickly by a soaking deluge.

"Stop." Vega's command freezes us where we are. We literally cannot move. Pax is frozen mid-stride, with one foot in the air. I'm amazed he doesn't topple over. Storm is hunched over in the act of reaching for one of the backpacks and Sky is leaning forward, just about to launch herself into a run. I'm happy to have both feet on the ground.

His voice changes again and releases us. "The ship is safe and there's much you need to know. Will you come with me?" Vega's hair blows wildly in the wind, but the rain isn't touching him. I understand why when I look up to see his ship hovering just above him. We're outside of its protective perimeter.

"No!" Storm shouts. "We don't trust you."

Sky says, "Wait, Storm. He could take us against our will, but he's asking." She turns to Vega, "Will you return us to this spot later? Will our memories be wiped?"

Vega smiles and Sky beams back. "We will return you shortly with your memories intact. We will also help Storm rescue his family."

I'm shivering. "Let's go, please. I want to be somewhere dry."

Vega snaps his fingers and the others gasp as they see the ship materialize. I feel vindicated. A portal opens and warm light spills out. That's when I remember to open my mental link to my dad.

Jewel? I hear him clearly.

Dad, we're going into an Allaran ship. I don't know if the link will work in there. Don't worry, I tell him.

Where are you? His thought sounds frantic. I should have known my saying 'don't worry' would give him an anxiety attack.

We're in a clearing in front of the sacred cave. Vega says he'll return us here. We'll be fine, Dad. I'll keep the link open.

We rise, one by one, into the light.

THIRTY-ONE

The portal opens in a small, round room lined with clear units that hold four spacesuits and a variety of equipment I don't recognize. We only get a quick look as Vega leads us to the next room. I don't know what I expected to see on the inside of an alien ship, but it wasn't this.

We stop short and can't help but gawk. We are surrounded by a living Caribbean reef, rich with a variety of sea creatures of all colors and shapes, swimming and crawling and doing what they naturally do. I feel Sky's delight as two bottlenose dolphins come to the wall, nod at us and flip around each other in a dolphin dance. The floor and ceiling soothe me with moving shades of blue and green. This could be the world's most beautiful aquarium if it wasn't in an alien spaceship.

Dad? I project. *Do you hear me?* He doesn't answer, but I promised to leave the link open. I expand the link in my mind to allow him to see through my eyes and hear through my ears, if he can.

Vega invites us to sit and I notice seven large, clear bubbles floating against one wall, inches from the floor. Each reflects the coral reef around us. No wonder I didn't see them before. Are we supposed to sit on them? In them? He demonstrates by sitting right where he is. One of the bubbles zips over to him and rises to meet him mid-squat. It folds around him, shapes itself to his body, and adds back and armrests.

Pax follows his lead and looks surprised to find himself in a comfortable chair. Storm hasn't stopped frowning, although I can't understand what's bothering him considering Vega's obvious hospitality and this gorgeous environment. Maybe Sky and I are under some sort of spell.

Once we're all settled, Vega says, "Terra is a tetra sphere." The reef fades away and we're suddenly adrift in space, looking at our beautiful planet from a distance. Floor, ceiling, walls have all become a viewport in which we float in our magic bubbles. Pax and Sky gasp as Storm lets out a growl, but I can't utter a sound. Wonder fills my soul as I watch the Earth rotating. Are we truly in space, or is this a projection? I'm afraid to ask.

A grid of interlocking triangles falls over the earth like a net and molds itself around the globe.

"The design you see represents actual lines of power that cover the planet. Some Terran scientists refer to the lines as a power grid and others call them ley lines. Still others give no credence to them at all. The triangles are actually three dimensional tetrahedra, each with four sides."

"The artifact is a tetrahedron," I interject. "Does it have anything to do with the grid?"

"Indeed," Vega answers. "Terra's organs follow the same geometric pattern as the planet itself. Creator made all the stars and planets as tetra spheres. In fact, the universe is one, as well as many universes that make up a tetra spherical multiverse."

"How do you know the universe is a tetra sphere? There's no geometric pattern to the location of stars, planets, or even galaxies," Pax replies. I hear genuine curiosity underlying the indignation his voice projects.

"The pattern is there, young Paxton. If you were to judge from what we see, imagine our viewpoint as that of a speck on an electron circling a nucleus. The atom, which is our solar system, is combined with others to form a cell, which would be our galaxy. If each galaxy is but a cell in, let's say, a human body, how can we possibly judge the complete body by what we see?

"Your scientists are making great strides in understanding how vast and complex our universe is. They now believe there are multiple universes, but have no way of measuring the size or shape of any of them, including ours.

"We have come much farther, and extrapolate the geometry of creation based on the measurements we know. It is endlessly fascinating, and we do not discount Creator's ability to surprise us and prove us wrong.

"None of what I've told you is relevant to your task, nor to the location and welfare of Sequoia and Wolf. I simply share knowledge with you that most Terrans do not yet have access to."

"Do you know where my family is?" Storm asks.

"Yes, Storm. We know. And we have a plan to retrieve them unharmed. Our plan requires us to wait until tonight. For now, I will return you to the clearing."

"I want to go with you when you get them," he says.

"So do I," Pax adds.

"Where Pax goes, I go," says Sky. I wish they hadn't spoken up. I haven't yet volunteered to do whatever needs doing in order to save the world, but I can't let my friends down.

"Count me in," I say, as an icy chill grips my stomach.

Vega raises his eyebrows and opens his eyes wide. "I am astonished, Star Children, that you are willing to do this. If you knew you were risking your lives, would you still want to come along?"

Storm and Pax jump to their feet and say in unison, "Yes." Their auras both flare brilliant red. It must be the color of courage and determination.

Sky and I look at each other. I feel tendrils of fear coming from her and I know she feels mine. Sky's aura has faded to pink, and I imagine a great yellow streak running down my back. We stand more slowly, grasp each other's hand and nod our heads. My heart says yes; my head disagrees.

"Very well," says Vega. His voice sounds satisfied. "Be outside of the Fletchers' home tonight at midnight. Together we will rescue Storm's family."

He leads us back to the portal room and the light lowers us gently to the wet ground. I watch the ship dart silently into the sky and take its place with the other three Sentinels. The storm has passed, and sunlight glints and dances prisms off droplets still falling from the trees.

Mom and Dad are waiting in the clearing. The dark look on Dad's face makes me think another storm is brewing. I hope we can eat something before it hits. Mom hears my stomach growl.

"You kids must be starving!" she exclaims. "You've been gone for hours. Follow us home and we'll have supper, and you can tell us all about it." She glares at Dad, daring him to open his mouth. He thinks better of letting loose with what's bothering him. The grimace on his face tells me how much the effort is costing him.

THIRTY-TWO

I ride home with my parents while the others head to the Fletcher's to shower and change. When we're nearly home, the silence becomes unbearable.

"I tried calling you from inside the ship, Dad. Did you hear me?"

"I did," he answers. His voice sounds strained. "I saw the aquarium switch to a view of Earth from space, and then everything stopped." He coughs and clears his throat.

Mom speaks up, "Your dad was beside himself, Jewel. He thought something terrible had happened to you and he couldn't help you. We were both so worried."

"They must be able to block the link from inside the ship," I say. "My ability worked fine in there. I saw the kids' auras and felt Sky's emotions, which means her ability also worked. Vega has no colors in his aura, but he does have a light around him."

"Is it like the life-force you see in animals?" Dad asks.

"No, it's more than that. It's ethereal, like the halos depicted in old paintings, but surrounding his body as well as his head. It dances like the northern lights. That's the best I can describe it."

"Mom and Dad?" I hesitate to bring this up, but remember how I felt when Vega first spoke to us. "The Watchers said both the Allarans and Dracans are the 'sons of God' mentioned in the Bible. They took human women as mates and produced offspring. When we met Vega, I felt a strong attraction to him, and I think Sky was feeling it too. He literally addled our brains. If he's typical of Allarans, I can see how they seduced human females. I can't imagine Dracans having that same effect, unless their disguises are so complete that women can't tell them from human men. If they have that ability, then why did they stop? Or did they?"

Dad makes choking sounds and the car swerves until Mom raps him sharply between his shoulder blades and he's able to take a deep breath. I wonder if he's coming down with something, or is he upset by what I said.

"Honey, you say you felt a strong attraction. Do you still feel it?" Mom asks.

"No. When he changed the tone of his voice, it faded, but didn't completely go away until we left the ship. I believe he has the ability to influence and even control people with his voice."

"I don't want you anywhere near those creatures." The way Dad says it reminds me of the belligerence that Storm and Pax had displayed. Do all men respond to Allarans this way? I don't say anything about our plan to meet them again tonight.

Neither Mom nor Dad answers my question about whether the aliens are still mating with humans or not. I guess they don't know, or perhaps they don't want to think about it.

As soon as we get home, I take a shower and change clothes while Mom prepares a quick dinner for us all. When the doorbell rings, Coral and Dylan come in with the twins and Storm.

Mom insists we eat our fill before talking about our experience, and we're all too happy to comply. After Storm clears the dishes and they've safely landed in the dishwasher I give him a nod.

"Storm, would you start by telling them what the Watchers said, please?"

Storm recounts the conversation we had with the Watchers, with frequent interruptions from the rest of us. We all heard the same voice saying the same thing, but we remember with slight variations. The bottom line is that our task is still ahead of us, and we still don't know when or how we'll accomplish it. I'm resigned to the fact that, voluntarily or not, I will do what needs to be done when the time comes.

Pax relays our meeting with Vega, while Storm glares silently. The boys had a very different experience from ours, and I'm sure it has to do with Vega's voice. I share my suspicions and Sky agrees.

In unspoken agreement, no one says anything about our plans for tonight. Storm tells the adults that the Allarans have a plot to rescue Wolf and Sequoia, but mentions nothing about our involvement.

Dad has calmed down considerably now that he knows everything that happened. He and the twin's father still share a knife-edged suspicion about the Allarans, but I can see that they're relieved that we didn't come to any harm.

I ask if I can spend the night with Sky, and our parents agree. I'd already packed an overnight bag after my shower, so I grab the bag and my keys and Sky and I take my car.

"When all this is over," she says, "I want to get a new red Mini Cooper."

"Hardtop or convertible?" I ask.

"Convertible. Definitely convertible, but with a strong roll-bar," she says and laughs. I'm glad she can laugh about it. I still shudder when I think of how close we came to losing her that night. Thank God Storm rescued her.

The others pull into the driveway behind us, and Coral and Dylan let us in and go straight to their room. We stay in our clothes and keep our jackets ready. There's no telling if the place we're going to is warm or cold, and we want to be prepared. When we've finished brushing our teeth, Sky turns on the television in her room. The boys come in and sprawl on the floor while we take Sky's bed, and we all watch the news.

*****

Breaking News: Major storms with blizzard conditions and multiple tornadoes are wreaking havoc along a stretch of the country from Texas all the way through Michigan. The weather system is rapidly moving east and will affect states from Alabama through New York tomorrow, and will hit the rest of the Eastern states on

Sunday. There is no sign that the storms will lose strength as they track across the country.

"Millions will be affected by power outages and can expect up to twelve inches of rain or three to six feet of snow in some places. Several governors have called for a state of emergency, and people are asked to stay indoors when the storms hit. Already, there have been multiple car accidents and fatalities. If you're in the path of these storms, you'll want to stock up on emergency supplies while you can. - Cayla Knox reporting for News Channel Twelve."

*****

"It looks like we're in for it, tomorrow." Pax runs his hand through his hair and yawns.

Storm yawns, too, and says, "I wonder if Allaran ships are affected by the weather? Will the storm system interfere in my folks' rescue?"

Sky and I both share a yawn. I hear the voice of the news announcer in my head, "Dangerous yawn contagion spreads among teenagers. Healthcare professionals urge quarantine for a period of at least eight hours if you notice any symptoms." At this point, I know I'm drifting off to sleep.

"Come on, Sky," I stand and pull on Sky's arm. "Let's get some instant coffee." I don't suggest real coffee because the smell would draw Coral out of her room. We need the caffeine, but we don't want parental intervention.

We heat up four mugs of water, add the coffee and bring a tray loaded with mugs, cream and sugar back to the room. Before we reach it I hear the snores. Sky sets the tray down on her desk, pours cream and sugar into her mug, and I settle back on the bed with my own warm mug. Pax is stretched out on his side on the floor next to me, his head facing the bed and lying on one arm. His long lashes rest on his cheek, and his relaxed mouth is slightly open and curves in a natural smile. I admire the strands of blond hair curling along his jaw. He snores softly and quietly, like a purring cat. My heart hammers and I'm glad for this moment. I sip more coffee.

Sky takes the other side of the bed, next to where Storm is lying on his stomach on the floor, head cradled in crossed arms. I see her regarding him much the same way I'm looking at Pax. I think we may both be smitten. The colors of her aura include flowing waves of red and pink when Storm is around. I wonder if mine is similar around Pax.

She sets the alarm for eleven-thirty in case we drift off, but the caffeine kicks in and we stay up watching television. A few minutes before the alarm is due to ring, I feel a tsunami of worry building higher and higher, threatening to crash over me and choke off my airway.

"Sky," I whisper and nudge her, "It will be fine. Everything will work out. It has to. We have to save the world, after all, and we can't do that if anything happens to us now."

"Do you really think so?" she asks. The wave ebbs a little, but she's still fearful. "I keep thinking about what Vega said about risking our lives. Why would they take us along if that's true? Don't they need us?"

"He didn't actually say we would be in danger. He asked if we would still volunteer if we knew our lives were at risk."

"Isn't that the same thing?" she asks, though I feel the anxiety lessen.

"Not really," I answer. "I think he was testing our resolve by that statement." I hope I'm right.

THIRTY-THREE

The alarm rings and Storm jumps up, startling us. Pax stretches and sits up more slowly. "Show time," he says, and his voice is calm. How does he do that? I'm already trembling from head to foot.

We put on jackets and shoes and head for the front door. Pax disarms the house alarm system, waits for us to get outside, re-arms it and joins us. We go to the side of the house away from Coral and Dylan's room and wait.

I shiver. The heat of early autumn days in North Carolina doesn't hint at how chilly the nights get. Heavy cloud cover blocks the moon and obscures the sky where I can usually see the Sentinels. When my eyes adjust to the dark, the life-force glow of millions of tiny critters casts a carpet of pale light over the grass in front of us. I see owls shining in the woods, and the light of a large cat slinks toward the deer that I can see as clearly as the cat does.

There, the ship hovers near the woods. "Follow me," I say and take the lead. Sky hangs on to my jacket, staying close with the boys right behind her.

Vega's glow outshines all the creatures in the woods. He's magnificent, like a tall, clothed statue of David. I feel my insides slowly melt. He hasn't spoken yet, so there's something other than his voice that holds power over me; that draws me like a moth to flame. That image jolts me out of it. If I think of him as a spider catching his supper in a web, I'll be less likely to be the supper. I realize Sky is feeling the same attraction.

"Snap out of it, Sky," I whisper, swatting at her. She drops back and I feel a wave of indignation. I also feel her strong emotions fade.

"Come, Star Children," Vega's voice has a commanding tone and we hurry to reach him. The light from the ship's portal momentarily blinds me, but I recover once we're inside the vessel. He leads us to the same room we were in before and instructs us to sit. I wonder who's piloting the ship.

The scene that surrounds us is a desert plain that sweeps up to craggy peaks bathed in the last rays of sunset, backed by a purple sky. The shape of the mountain resembles the broken-off teeth of a giant human mandible. Where the orange-red rays of the sun hit, the 'teeth' stand out, jagged and sharp; I'm struck by the harsh beauty before me.

"Superstition Mountain, in Arizona," Vega announces. "We will be there shortly."

Storm is impatient and asks, "When do we start moving?"

Vega laughs, and Storm and Pax both stiffen in their seats. "We're more than half-way there," he says. "Our propulsion system is silent, and there is no air friction because the skin of our ship produces an energy field that slips through both air and water without resistance."

"I've heard there are legends about that mountain; something about a gold mine and a hole to the underworld." I remember reading about it a few years ago.

"Yes," Vega says. "The Dracans have lived in a city underneath the mountain for eons, and the Apache who settled in that part of the country were aware of their comings and goings. The humans believed the entrance to the underground city was an opening to the netherworld, which, in a sense, it is. They considered it holy ground.

"Later, when settlers came from the east, an explorer entered one of their mine tunnels and found a storage room of Dracan gold. He was discovered, but escaped to tell others about the mine. He refused to divulge its location and never returned himself, but his tale led to an invasion of prospectors that ended when many disappeared. Thus the legend of the Lost Dutchman's Mine was born. Even today, the Apache say that the Thunder God protects the mine and avoid the area."

"That's all very interesting," Storm interrupts, "but what can we expect when we get there? Do you have a plan to rescue my family, and what can we do to help?"

"Yes," Vega answers. "My apologies, Storm. I know you are worried about them. We have some allies among the Dracans; those who believe what we have told them about the artifacts. They have lived on this planet long enough to consider it their home and do not wish to see it destroyed. It is in their best interest to aid us. They will meet us at the mountain with Sequoia and Wolf. The time may come when we will have further need of their assistance, and they ours, particularly if they are discovered."

Sky sounds relieved when she asks, "Does that mean we won't have to risk our lives?"

"Not this time, Little One." I expect an indignant backlash from Sky at the name, but she remains calm and happy.

"We have arrived," Vega announces, and we move to the portal room. He exits first and we wait until he calls us.

Storm rocks from foot to foot because there isn't room enough to pace. I understand his nervous energy, but wish he'd stay still while we're crowded in here. No one speaks until we hear Vega's call, and Storm immediately steps into the light and disappears through the portal. Pax goes next, followed by Sky and finally me.

The desert is pitch-black outside of the portal light. Unlike in the meadows around our houses in North Carolina, the wildlife here is too scattered to illuminate anything. I feel a bit disoriented until I look up. A dome of stars covers the sky from horizon to horizon; billions upon billions of stars and galaxies are visible and sparkling. The Milky Way stretches like a highway to heaven and I remember Vega's comparison of galaxies to cells. How infinitesimally small we are.

Shapes materialize out of the desert, two standing upright and two on floating stretchers. The Dracans are more imposing than I remember; taller and more muscular. Their eyes glow green until they enter the light and I see that they're yellow with vertical pupils, like cat eyes, and the skin on their faces and hands is scaled. I can't see what color they are in the darkness, but I do see that they have no auras.

The stretchers gently float to the ground and Storm rushes over to touch his aunt and uncle.

"Sequoia? Wolf?" he calls their names but they don't answer. He turns to the tallest Dracan and demands, "What have you done to them?"

"They are in stasis, young Storm. No harm has befallen them." His voice is deep and both guttural and sibilant, and he exposes rows of sharp teeth as he speaks. I wonder how he knows Storm's name. Does he know ours, too?

Vega instructs Storm, "Float them to the portal and we will take them home." We follow the stretchers and Vega stays behind to speak to the Dracans. The door to the viewing room is open when we enter the ship. Storm floats his aunt and uncle in and lowers them to the floor. They appear to be sleeping peacefully. Pax checks their pulse and nods. Sky sinks to the floor between them and lays a hand on each of their heads, and I feel the peace and love she's sending them.

When Vega returns, the view switches back to the Fletchers' house, dark and silent. Then it changes to Storm's cabin and we see the porch light is on.

"We will see that Sequoia and Wolf are returned to their bed," Vega assures us. "They will remember nothing. It is your choice whether to tell them that they were abducted, or not. We do not know what they experienced among the Dracans. I am sorry, but they told me nothing."

Storm stands and faces Vega. "Thank you, Vega, and the crew of this ship. I won't forget this."

"No gratitude is needed, Storm. If we survive, we will all owe you and your companions a debt of gratitude we will never be able to repay."

THIRTY-FOUR

SKY

I sit between Sequoia and Wolf and send them positive energy until we reach their cabin. It seems like the trip took minutes, but I'm so focused on them I can't be sure. There is no feedback of emotion, so I assume they're in some kind of coma. I'm unaware that we've arrived until Storm puts his hands on my shoulders.

"We're here, Sky. Thank you." His touch sends an unexpected current running through me, and his voice, warm and deep, is like hot chocolate and honey to my spirit. He's dangerous, I remind myself. Besides, I'm pretty sure he likes Jewel. I feel increased intensity in him when she's around.

But what about the day I was attacked, when Jewel wasn't there? I shove the thought down and stand up. He floats Wolf's stretcher to the portal room while we stay with Sequoia. Vega goes with him. A few minutes later, he returns for his aunt.

"I'll stay here with them," he says. "Vega will take you back to the Fletchers' place."

Pax assures him, "I'll tell my parents that you got a call that they're home. They'll understand why you aren't there in the morning."

Seconds after Vega returns he informs us that we're at our house. I have never felt this tired and can't wait to get to bed. Pax opens the door, resets the alarm and we stagger to our rooms. Jewel plops down on one side of my bed and I take the other. I remember nothing else until Mom wakes us up.

~~~~

"Okay, girls." Her voice is loud enough to wake the dead. I pull my pillow over my ears. She pulls it off. "It's nearly time for lunch and you all have to eat something. Get up, please." She leaves and I hear her knock on Pax's door.

Jewel stretches and yawns loudly beside me. "Do you realize we slept in our clothes?" she asks. "I wonder if your mom noticed."

"Oh, she noticed," I tell her. "Nothing gets by Mom. We'll hear about it over lunch."

Jewel showers first and by the time I've showered and dressed, I'm starving and Jewel is already in the kitchen helping Mom set the table and put the food out.

Pax comes in, unshaven and with his hair still wet from the shower. "Where's Dad?"

Mom waits until we're seated. She prays over the food, passes around plates of cheese and sandwich meat and a basket of rolls, and then says, "Wolf called this morning and Dad drove right over. He was surprised to see that Storm was already gone. Do you know anything about that?"

Pax speaks up, "Storm heard they'd returned late last night and went home. I hope they're alright."

It isn't a lie. Hearing is one of the senses, and all of Storm's senses were engaged in our rescue last night, so he did hear. They did return and he did go home. Pax winks at me. I swear he reads my mind sometimes.

"May I ask why you were all fully dressed when I woke you up this morning?"

Again Pax answers, "We went outside with Storm and saw him off. It was late and we were tired enough to crash when we came back inside." His answer seems to satisfy her.

"After we eat," Mom says, "we'll pack up some food and bring it over to them. I imagine Sequoia won't want to cook for a while. I wonder where they were."

Jewel looks like she's about to say something but I send her a warning nudge. It isn't exactly mind-speech, but she gets it and turns her attention to her sandwich. We're getting better at this silent communication, even without her dad's wristbands.

We listen to Mom chatter while we clean up and pack the food in plastic bags.

"Jewel, your parents are going over. You can ride home with them later. Get your jackets on. It's cold, windy and wet outside."

When we get to the porch, the forest is loud with creaking trees whipping back and forth in the wind. Rain comes down in sheets, as if a giant faucet has been opened full-force in the sky above us. Umbrellas are no match for the wind and we throw dripping bags of food into the back of Pax's SUV. We're soaked to the skin by the time we climb into the car. He turns up the heat and fights the buffeting wind as we take the curvy road to the cabin.

Getting out of the car into a muddy yard is even more challenging. Lightning strikes nearby and a giant clap of thunder motivates us to hurry into the cabin. Dad comes out dressed in a plastic poncho that nearly trips him up when the wind whips it around his legs. He grabs the food bags from the back of the SUV and runs into the house just as a bolt of lightning hits a tree across the yard.

"That's enough excitement for me, today," Jewel announces. I agree with her.

We hang up our jackets and Jewel and I follow Mom into the kitchen where we unpack the bags of food while she goes to hug Sequoia. Pax heads to the living room where Storm and his aunt and uncle are talking with Dad. The front door flies open and Jewel's drenched parents shake droplets off their jackets and wipe muddy shoes on the welcome mat. Charles picks up a pack he'd set down and goes straight to the living room.

We carry trays into the living room and join the boys on the floor near the wall. Storm feels at peace for once, but I detect an undercurrent of tension rising as Jewel slides down next to Pax. My teeth clench and I move to sit next to Storm. I hope my own tension doesn't affect him. He's been through enough. Sequoia and Wolf look none the worse for their ordeal.

Wolf tells the story once everyone has eaten something and Storm has finished his increasingly popular dish dance to the dishwasher. I feel his self-satisfaction and our moms' admiration and wish I could clean up that way.

"We were going to stock up on supplies in town. All we remember is walking through the yard and then waking up in bed. Everything between is a blank. Storm told us about the search and that the Allarans rescued us from the Dracans."

Mom gives me a surprised look. I feel her confusion, and shake my head while I push peace toward her. I wonder if Storm mentioned that we went along for the rescue.

Sequoia dispels my concern. "Storm was here when we woke up, thinking nothing had happened. He said he'd been staying at the Fletchers' house when the Allarans let him know we'd returned. Thank you, Coral and Dylan, for keeping our nephew with you while we were missing." There are tears in her eyes.

I shoot Storm a grateful look and I'm surprised to find him looking at me intently. Oh, I could so easily get lost in those amber eyes of his. They sparkle with flecks of gold and I can't tear my gaze away. It doesn't help that he doesn't look away either. There's that strange tension again. I try not to think that what he's feeling is directed at me. What if I'm wrong and he really likes Jewel? I couldn't bear it, so I refuse to get my hopes up. It takes effort, but I turn my attention to the adults. Is that disappointment coming from him, or from me?

Charles reaches into a pack and pulls out something that makes my heart speed up. He holds a wristband in his hand and lays it on the coffee table. Is it possible that they're ready?

THIRTY-FIVE

Charles quickly returns it to the pack when a loud knock interrupts what he was about to say. Storm jumps up to answer it and returns, tailed by Sheriff Green. Is it my imagination or does Storm deliberately brush against my arm and sit closer than before? The brief contact sends delicious shivers through me. Stop, Sky, I tell myself, but my body isn't listening to me.

Wolf repeats his story to the sheriff, who writes in an official looking notebook.

"When you left the house," he asks, "did you notice anything in the sky above you? Was there a shadow or any indication that a Dracan ship was around?"

"We didn't notice anything at all, Sheriff," Wolf explains. "And we have no recollection of anything that happened after that moment until we woke up here."

"Are there any marks on you?" Sheriff Green persists. "Do you feel different in any way?"

Sequoia speaks up, "Are you suggesting that they might have experimented on us, Sheriff?"

"I have no idea," the Sheriff shakes his head, "but we're dealing with a complete unknown here and any information would give us a better picture of what these aliens want."

We know what they want, I'm thinking, but we don't know what they did to Storm's family.

"We have found no marks and we feel fine," Wolf answers the Sheriff. I see a look in Sequoia's eyes and feel a wave of anxiety from her that indicates he isn't telling the whole truth. Why not?

The sheriff's radio squawks and he gets up and goes to answer it in the kitchen before heading out the front door. The wind seems to have died down and I don't hear the pounding rain. Charles goes to the window to be sure he's gone and reaches once more into the pack when he returns to his seat.

"Before I tell you about this wristband, kids, you need to agree that everything we discuss here must stay among us. You cannot breathe one word about this to anyone else, human or otherwise. Do you understand?"

I nod and the boys each say 'Yes, sir' aloud. Our folks don't know that we've known about the wristbands since Jewel told me and I spilled the beans to the boys.

Charles continues, "Analiese and I have developed one of these for each of you, including the twins' parents and Storm's folks. They will give you the ability to speak telepathically with each other."

None of the adults are surprised and they all look at us as if they expect us to be.

"They know," Jewel says.

Charles gives her a look that promises they will discuss this later, and continues, "The way it has worked for us is that we can call Jewel and each other, and she can call either or both of us. It's a three-way connection that can be activated and deactivated by any one of us at any time.

"Adding you three kids and your folks has made it much more complex. The only way Analiese and I have been able to make it happen is to make the four of you the primary link, and to limit our links to our own kids."

"Will we be able to call each other individually, without everyone listening in?" Storm asks.

"Yes. You four will have instant access to each other by pressing on the button at the edge of the screen where it meets the band. Either edge will do. Then quickly tap twice for Storm, three times for Pax, four times for Sky and five times for Jewel."

Pax asks, "What happens if we only tap once?"

Charles smiles, "One tap will link all of you together. You might want to use that one judiciously."

Analiese walks us through the signals we'll be using to contact our folks. "Remember not to press the buttons to call your parents. For simplicity's sake, you'll use the Morse code "M" for Mom and "D" for Dad. Sorry, Storm, but it's the same for you." He nods and smiles.

To speak to both, simply tap out one followed by the other. You break the connection by pressing on the screen for two full seconds."

"What if we can't talk when someone calls? We could be in the middle of something," Pax says.

"You say you're busy and end the connection. Just remember that if someone calls, a response is absolutely required. If you don't answer, we have to act on the assumption that something has happened to prevent you from answering. Our emergency protocol will activate."

I ask, "What emergency protocol?"

Charles points to a button on the side of the device farthest from the hand. "This button turns the screen on or off and activates the fitness monitor. The button on the opposite side activates an emergency signal to the four of you and to the set of parents associated with the one who presses it. We have a similar button that notifies all of the parents when you're in trouble."

It all sounds terribly complicated to me. We'll have to memorize the code and practice using the wristbands. The thought occurs to me and I ask, "What if we lose it?"

"They're designed to stay on," Charles explains. "Analiese and I have the special code required to release them from your wrists. We'll share it with your folks, but you won't have access to it. I'm afraid once you put them on, they'll remain on your wrists. They're waterproof and loose enough not to chafe. They're made of a special chemical alloy given to us by the Watchers and can't be broken."

Jewel has already explained it to us, but Storm asks anyway, "Will anyone be able to read our minds whenever they want?"

Charles looks into Storm's eyes and softens his voice, "No, son. Your thoughts are private and no one will be able to invade your privacy.

These wristbands make it possible for you to speak to each other at will, nothing more." Storm nods and I feel him relax.

It's too bad. It would be fascinating to eavesdrop on his thoughts, especially when I feel that tension rise in him.

I see Jewel drop her head and notice her finger tapping on her band. I look around to see whether she's talking to her mom or dad. Charles shakes his head almost imperceptibly, and by the time I look back at Jewel, she's pressing on the band. I wonder what that's about. She doesn't feel upset, so I dismiss it.

THIRTY-SIX

Analiese and Charles attach a band to each of our wrists. Mine is a lovely soft cream color that feels like doeskin, like Jewel's, although hers is a slightly darker tan. I'm happy to see that the wristbands are different from each other. Pax's is a deep royal blue and looks like leather. Storm's is predictably black and also leather-looking.

For the next hour we practice using the codes. I'm happy to discover we sound like we always do without the annoying buzz we get from the Watchers. Hearing someone else's voice in my head doesn't bother me at all. I listen to my own all day, and now I don't have to make up conversations. I share that with Jewel and her mind-laugh echoes through my brain in a delightful way. The boys annoy us by saying *Testing...Testing* over and over again.

At least Jewel has something to say. *Are you okay with this Sky?*

I can get used to it, I answer. *It'll come in handy when we have something to gossip about and don't want anyone overhearing us.* She laughs again. I love this.

After we've all had a chance to speak to our parents, and Storm to his aunt and uncle, Pax says out loud, "Why don't we four go to the store and pick up some supplies?"

Dad agrees, "That's a great idea. We can practice using the bands from a distance."

The weather has cleared considerably, although it's still windy and the sky is full of racing gray clouds. We pile into Pax's SUV and he says, "I don't want to be tapping on this thing while I'm driving. Let's just talk normally, okay?"

We agree and drive into town. Mom calls me as soon as we leave, and I see by his frown that she's contacted Pax, too. *I just wanted to see if I can contact both of you,* she says.

I hear Pax's response, *I'm busy driving, Mom,* and he presses on the face of his monitor. It leaves Mom and me to speak to each other. We chat for a few minutes and break the connection. I hope she and Dad don't overuse this mind-speak.

The Blue Mountain grocery store is more like a general store, offering everything from clothes and toys to electronics; from books to frozen dinners and fresh vegetables.

"Sequoia deliberately didn't give me a list," Storm says as Pax parks the car. "She wants to link and tell me what to get as we wander the aisles."

"How will she know which aisle you're in?" asks Pax, always the logical one. We climb out of the car and start walking toward the store.

"You can open your mind to her," Jewel says quietly and looks around to make sure we're out of anyone's hearing range. "She'll see what you see and hear what you hear."

My mouth drops open. "Your dad didn't say anything about that." The three of us stop and stare at her.

"It's something we discovered the first time Vega took us into his ship," she explains. "Dad saw everything until just after we saw the image of the revolving Earth. The link cut off after that, and we think the Allarans have a way of blocking it."

The store is nearly empty, and only a handful of other shoppers wander the aisles.

Storm taps on his wristband and grabs a shopping cart. I grab another out of habit, glad for something to hold on to. He turns toward me and I see his eyes widen. He feels pleased about something, but I'm afraid to tap into his conversation in case it interferes with his connection. He's soon adding one thing after another to the cart. Besides groceries, he adds a pile of first aid items and a couple of blankets. When his cart fills up, he adds items to mine.

Sky?

I hear you, Jewel, I answer.

It looks like it's working, doesn't it? The stuff he's getting is what my mom would put on a list for me. I nod without answering.

My thoughts drift to Storm and how domestic he looks shopping. I admire the fit of his black leather jacket and the way his muscular legs fit his jeans.

You're projecting, Jewel interrupts my thoughts. *Don't forget you need to end the connection.* Her laughter takes the sting out of her reminder. Maybe we can't read each other's minds, but we can pick up on thoughts if they're loud enough. How do you turn the volume down on thoughts? Thank God I didn't interrupt Storm's conversation with his aunt. A hot blush rushes into my face at the thought of what they would have overheard if I had.

I press on the face of the fitness monitor and smile at Jewel. Having a friend like her is amazing.

We stop at the gun display where Wild Bill Stern is working on a laptop sitting on the counter. He's one of the tribal elders and the owner of the store.

"What can I do for you today, Storm?" His words sound cheerful, but there's a deep furrow between his eyebrows and the lines around his mouth give him a grim look. His mouth smiles, but his eyes don't.

Storm asks for boxes of ammo for three different rifles Wolf keeps at home for hunting. "How's your family, Mr. Stern?" he asks politely.

"Fine. Fine," he seems distracted as he fetches the ammo and hands it to Storm. "I heard your folks turned up safe and sound. Glad to hear it. Give them my regards, will you?"

Storm nods and we continue down the aisle. I tap Jewel. *Something is wrong. Do you feel it?*

No, but Mr. Stern's colors are muddy and dull. He's really worried about something.

I wish we could read his mind, I think.

I don't, Jewel answers. *We have enough to worry about. I doubt if Mr. Stern is supposed to save the world. He could be concerned about the tunnel the Dracans dug on his property.*

That must be it, I answer.

Marla Snow comes around the shelves at the end of the aisle. Max rounds the corner right behind her. Great. I notice some of Max's other friends, the 'Lost Boys', roaming around the store and wonder what they're doing here on a Saturday afternoon. Shouldn't they be home in this weather?

"Well, well, if it isn't the four mouseketeers," Max bellows. He acts as if he hasn't been working with us to figure out the mystery of the boreholes. His friends loan him courage, I suppose, and the bravado is his way of establishing his alpha position in the group. I press the button near the band and tap once. *Let's just leave,* I project.

Not until I pay for the supplies. Storm's anger pounds in my brain. It seems thoughts convey more emotion than our voices. Oh, this is not good at all for me.

I'm right behind you, Storm. I feel Pax's readiness to jump in and fight. I wonder if there's therapy available for an empath like me.

Don't worry, Sky. These bozos aren't going to fight, are you, boys? Storm is going to pay and we're getting out of here.

Max and his friends close in until a can flies off the shelf and hits his arm.

"Ouch!" he yelps. "Cut it out, Storm! We don't mean any harm."

"That's good to know, Max. You know I don't mess around." I wonder why Max continues to challenge him like this. Does Marla have anything to do with it? I see her by the checkout lane, a self-satisfied smirk on her face. What is she up to?

There is no line, so checkout is quick and we load the supplies into the back of the SUV. I hear the rumble of distant thunder. There's more rain coming.

THIRTY-SEVEN

The rumble grows into a roar and I'm thrown off my feet as the ground heaves. "Pax!" my voice is lost in the crash of noise. I throw my arms over my head and curl into a fetal ball. A steadying arm circles around me and I feel myself drawn close to a hard chest.

"Hold on, Sky!" Storm's voice shouts near my ear. The ground moves furiously, like a living thing beneath us. When it finally calms, I feel brokenness all around. Terror flails at me from all sides. Fear, pain, grief, confusion; I struggle to push them away. Where is Pax?

Storm's arms tighten around me and I feel the frantic pounding of his heart match my own. Concern for him overwhelms me and pushes against the onslaught of countless silent cries for help so that I can focus on him. I allow my feelings to flow into him, mine and no one else's, and feel his heart slow into normal rhythm. I feel his wonder in return.

Storm lets me go and we pull ourselves upright on the broken pavement and look for the others. Jewel is sitting on an intact piece of the curb, cradling Pax's bloody head in her lap. Tears track through the dust and mud on her face and for a second, my heart stops.

A jagged gash starts just above his eyebrow and disappears into his hairline, still bleeding freely. He's alive, but unconscious. Storm finds the bag with first aid supplies in the car and comes back with gauze and bandages. Jewel helps me apply pressure to the wound with the gauze while we wrap the bandage around it. After Storm floats him to the back seat and covers him with a blanket, he runs to what used to be the store.

"I want to stay with him," Jewel says. I do too, but people are in trouble all around us.

"Jewel, he'll be fine. I'll know when he wakes up. We have to help the folks around here."

She touches his face, straightens her spine and turns to me. "Okay. Let's go."

I see her tap her wristband and I do the same. We let our parents know what happened and that we're fine but Pax is injured. *We'll call an ambulance,* Mom says, her fear evident.

The road is all torn up, Mom. The bleeding is under control and he's resting in the car. I'll be here when he wakes up and I'll let you know. Are all of you okay?

She answers, *the quake rattled us quite a bit, but we're fine. We're heading toward town right now.*

I send love and end the connection. Jewel and I shove some of the first aid supplies in our pockets and gingerly make our way to the store.

The two-story building has pancaked into one story, with rubble completely covering the door and front windows. Storm telekinetically lifts large blocks of cement and plaster and opens a passage into the interior. I'm surprised to see that display shelves and steel beams have left wide pockets of space where people found shelter. Max is among the group closest to the cleared passage and rushes outside, a look of sheer panic on his face. Storm gently lifts an injured woman, unable to put weight on her foot, and floats her through the opening to the street outside, where he lowers her to a clear patch of sidewalk. A young mother picks up her toddler and scrambles out of the rubble.

I feel the pain and fear of people still trapped inside. If I can just focus on one at a time, I'll be able to help locate them. There. The closest one is near the cash registers to our left.

I tap the wristband and open our link. *Storm. The checkout clerk is still alive. Can you get us to her?*

He shoves debris out of the way and Jewel spots her, nearly obscured by dust and chunks of fallen ceiling. *Her aura is faint.*

She's unconscious and after clearing rubble off her, Storm airlifts her outside. The street is filling up with people, and a paramedic stops to help the clerk.

We spend what feels like hours clearing pathways and helping people out of the building. We find Wild Bill behind the largely untouched gun display where he'd ducked when the shelves started swaying. As soon as Storm clears the way for him he pitches in and helps free the others. When I can't sense anyone else, and Jewel can't find another life force, she asks, *do you think Marla made it out okay?*

She probably slithered through the nearest hole, I say, and then immediately feel guilty for putting her down. I can't feel her emotions, but she's probably scared right now, if she isn't dead.

Storm talks to the paramedic I saw earlier and Jewel and I leave to check on Pax. The car door is open, and he isn't there. Our link is still open, but Pax hasn't checked in. *PAX?*

Not so loud, Sky. My head is killing me.

Jewel laughs out loud and I share her intense relief. *Where are you?* And then I feel him right behind me. I turn and hug him tightly. "Do Mom and Dad know you're alright?"

"I let them know as soon as I remembered how to use the bracelet," he says. "Everything was fuzzy for a while. I figured you guys bandaged me up and got me into the car. I've been looking for you."

"You could have called any time. The link has been open."

"I didn't want to interfere in your rescue operation. Nice work." He reaches for Jewel and hugs her. I feel the warmth between them and turn my attention to the people in the street around us.

I end the connection with the others and check in with Mom. *Pax woke up and he's fine, Mom. Do you know how strong this quake was?*

It wasn't a quake, sweetheart. A large chunk of mountain broke off and slid into the valley. It obliterated a large section of road, and we can't get to you. Let the others know we're all fine up here. The newscasters are saying the rains and recent earthquakes, caused the break in the mountain, but we know better. Sheriff Green told Wolf that the rift exposed some of the Dracans' tunnels.

We'll get there as soon as we can. The road may not be passable, but we have Storm. Give Dad and the others our love in the meantime. I break the connection with Mom and reconnect with Pax and the others and tell them what happened.

We pile into the car and Storm maneuvers around tossed vehicles and rough cracks in the pavement. He floats us over sinkholes and the worst of the wreckage and we're soon out of town and heading toward home. A cloud of dust hangs in the air over the remains of the mountain ahead. It reminds me of lava flowing down a valley during a volcanic eruption; only the valley has been newly cut by the mountain itself. Boulders jut out of a sea of mud. Ruined tree trunks poke out everywhere like giant broken toothpicks. The massive destruction sends a sharp pain through my heart and my eyes burn with unshed tears. Jewel grabs my hand and her sorrow compounds mine. We're each lost in our own thoughts and forget that the connection is still open.

Emergency vehicles with flashing lights block the road ahead. We pull over, park behind Sheriff Green's car and go look for him. A deputy directs us to the brink of the new crater.

"Stay away from the edge. It's dangerous." He says, as if we need to be reminded.

A sharp-edged chasm separates the broken edge of the road from the strangely altered land. We find the sheriff talking to a deputy who is snapping photos of the destruction. He excuses himself and comes over to us.

"Storm. Pax. Girls. Your folks told me you were in town when it happened."

"We were in Wild Bill's store," Storm says. "We got him out and he helped us dig out a bunch of other people. Sheriff, do you know what caused this? Off the record."

"I suspect the Dracan tunneling destabilized the mountain. All this rain loosened it and sent it tumbling. More rain's coming. Flash flooding will be as dangerous as this, especially in the hollers. Think you might lend a hand if we need it?"

"Of course. We all will. Pax is really good at tracking; Jewel sees the light surrounding people and Sky can feel their emotions. Pax was out of commission for a while, but the rest of us found everyone in the store by using our gifts."

"I see Pax has recovered. We'll count on you kids. There's a back road you can take across this mess farther up the mountain. I'll instruct my guys to let you through."

"You know I can fly us over the chasm," Storm laughs.

"Not here, you won't," Sheriff Green says without so much as cracking a smile. "Up the mountain and out of sight, you can do whatever you want."

THIRTY-EIGHT

PAX

I'm exhausted and the cut on my head has changed from throbbing to sharp stabs of pain in spite of Sky's attempts to send soothing feelings. I need the medicine woman, and soon. Whatever she did to speed Storm's and Sky's recovery, I hope she can do for me.

I can't believe how much of the mountain just slid away like that. Thank God there were no cabins in that part of the forest, or we might be counting bodies. Safety is an illusion in this day and age on the now unstable planet. I wonder when we'll be called to fix the artifact. If and when we do fix it, will it be enough to settle things down? How many of them are there? Are they all sick? Earth looked nice and small while we were in the Allaran ship, but as tiny as we humans are in comparison, this is a big planet. It hurts to think, so I close my eyes as soon as we get to the car.

Storm takes the wheel again and heads up the trail the deputy pointed out to us. It's steep and winds through the forest. When we reach a bend that's close to the break and we're out of sight of the emergency vehicles, he jumps us over the chasm. In short order, we're pulling up to his cabin where Wolf, Charles, and Dad are waiting in the yard. They greet the girls with hugs and Charles walks with them to the house. I try to get out of the car, but my legs seem to have lost their strength and I quickly drop back to the seat. Dad and Wolf come over to help me. Wolf puts an arm around my waist on one side, and Dad does the same on the other. I throw my arms across their shoulders, and I'm grateful for the support, I'm feeling pretty dizzy.

I could fly you in, Storm suggests.

Thanks, but I think Dad wants to feel useful. Maybe next time. Storm grins at that and cuts the connection. I'll bet he hopes there is a next time.

The ladies have a hot meal ready for us in the kitchen. The smell of food is making me a bit queasy, so Dad helps me into one of the recliners in the living room and goes to make me some tea. Sequoia comes in carrying a bowl of some kind of paste. I hope I don't have to eat it. Wolf places a basin of hot water and some clean cloth on the coffee table.

"I'm going to unwrap the bandage and clean your wound, Pax," she says in a calming voice. I'm growing to love this medicine woman aunt of Storm's. She smoothly unwinds the bandage and then quickly rips off the gauze that's stuck to the cut. My teeth clench in reflex to the pain and I hear myself groan. Sky feels that I'm hurting, and sends a quick wave of peace from the kitchen.

Sequoia dabs the cloth in the basin and cleans the cut. The hot water burns for a second and then brings warm relief. Her touch is gentle and she hums a soft Cherokee song as she works. As soon as she's satisfied, she reaches for the paste.

"I hope you're biting on a stick, brother," Storm says as he walks in gnawing on a chicken leg. "That stuff is murder."

"Go back to the kitchen," Sequoia says sharply. "Pax will be fine."

I discover I might want that stick when my head erupts in fire as soon as the paste touches it. I yelp and hear Storm's answering laugh, and then all pain abruptly stops and my vision blurs. *Nap time,* I hear his voice in my head, and then nothing.

~~~~

I don't know how I got there, but I wake up on the couch in our living room at home. Sky is curled up near my feet watching television. Mom and Dad are here, too, in their chairs. How much time has passed?

The normalcy of this scene feels surreal, considering the mess the town is in.

Welcome back, Sky says in my head. *How do you feel?*

I squint a little until my eyes adjust to being awake. Mom pauses the TV and the three of them look at me. "How are you feeling?" Dad asks.

I struggle to sit up and find that my head doesn't hurt and the dizziness is gone. "Sequoia is a miracle worker," I tell them. "I feel like I've slept for days. Have I?"

Mom laughs, "You've been asleep a few hours. But we should all go to bed as soon as the news is over." I settle back and we watch footage of our local disaster together.

*****

Breaking News: "Heavy rains coupled with recent minor earthquakes caused a mountainside to collapse in Blue Mountain, North Carolina, this afternoon. An unpopulated area of forested land, more than a hundred yards across, cut through the mountain highway as it slid hundreds of feet into the valley below. The force of the slide caused a quake that collapsed buildings in town a mile away and buckled roadways for at least two miles in every direction. Power is out all over the area and there's no telling how long before crews can restore it. No deaths have been reported, so far. Rescue workers and residents are digging through the rubble searching for survivors. We'll have updates as more reports come in.

"Another wave of strong storms is expected to bring up to twelve inches of rain to the mountains in eastern Tennessee and western North Carolina. Flash flood warnings have been issued and residents are urged to find shelter away from creeks and rivers.

"In other news: A mile-wide F-5 tornado tore through the outskirts of Oklahoma City early this morning, devastating a six-mile stretch of neighborhoods and destroying at least two schools.

Thankfully, the schools were unoccupied. At least ten people have died and many more are injured. It is not known at this time how many people are missing. The number of casualties is expected to rise as residents search through the debris. - Cole Porter here, reporting for News Channel Six."

*****

"Wait a minute," I break in. I'm confused. "Did he say the power is out? How are we watching this? How is our power still on?"

Sky gives me a questioning look, as if the thought hadn't crossed her mind until now.

"You've heard of electromagnetism, haven't you, Pax?" Mom asks. "Earth is a generator, of sorts, and produces a form of usable energy. Nikola Tesla had the right idea, that there is limitless free energy that can be transmitted remotely throughout the world. He wasn't able to develop it, thanks to human greed, but our alien friends have known about it and used it for thousands of years."

"Does it have anything to do with ley lines?" Sky asks. She paid attention when Vega showed us the energy grid in the form of interlocking tetrahedra.

"The ley lines, or energy grid, are like superhighways of electromagnetism. Maximum power is found where they interconnect. Your dad and I have devised instruments that measure and track the power grid. There's an especially strong junction just north of Clingman's Dome, and our power is drawn from that point where the ley lines cross."

Sky stands to her feet, and stretches. "You're saying alien technology gives us power even during a blackout that's caused by severed lines. Exactly how much of our house is alien? Are Storm and Jewel's homes powered the same way?"

Mom gets up and stretches, followed by Dad. "Alien technology was used to build our homes, with the exception of the O'Connell cabin. Wolf and Sequoia built their home out of logs. Dan Jones and his company, Blue Mountain Construction, used regular building materials bonded with an alien compound on ours. The windows, walls, roof, floor and basement all contain that compound, which makes the house nearly impermeable to any kind of attack. You saw how the beam of light from the Dracan ship had no effect on Jewel's house."

"Does that mean Storm's house is vulnerable?" I ask.

"No," Dad answers. "The Allarans have covered his home in a clear shield of the same compound. All of our homes have power. It's unlimited and free, and once the artifacts are working properly, I have permission to share this technology with anyone who wants it."

"Is that a good idea, Dad?" I ask. "Remember what happened to Tesla. His funding was cut off and his transmission tower destroyed. Free energy will cause an economic disaster."

"At first, perhaps," Dad says. "Once it's put into use, though, the economy would quickly recover. I'm sure the power brokers will find some other way to amass their fortunes.

"Right now, it's time for bed. We need to get our rest tonight. The storms we're expecting tomorrow will wreak havoc in these mountains. The ground is already saturated, and creeks are running high as it is. Sheriff Green has been trying to evacuate the folks living in the hollers, but they're a stubborn lot and many won't leave their cabins. We'll all have to do what we can to help out. Since our houses are safe, we, along with the Adams and O'Connells, will prepare to shelter as many people as we can. We have plenty of supplies and cots stored in the subbasement."

I say goodnight and get ready for bed, but I don't sleep. I hardly feel the wound on my head, but my thoughts spin circles around me; thoughts of free energy, reptilian aliens, silver spacecraft, sick artifacts, a wobbly planet, and Jewel. Especially Jewel.

I drift off thinking of her and she's running from a monster with Storm's face. He rips her away from me, and I chase him through a midnight forest crawling with giant lizards that grab at my clothes and trip me while the monster disappears with Jewel in his arms. I somehow catch up to him and beat him to the ground and pull her to me. In my dream, she's mine.

THIRTY-NINE

I wake up to loud bangs at the front door and commotion in the house. My alarm clock says it's nine. Apparently, my folks let me sleep in because it's obvious from the sounds that they've been up a while. Mom knocks at the door and comes in.

"Pax, grab your rain gear and pack up some clothes. You and Sky are staying with the Adams tonight and we'll be using your rooms for some of the families. Breakfast is in the kitchen. Make sure you eat well. It'll be a long day. Bring plenty of water and snacks with you."

The kitchen and living room are teeming with bedraggled women. Some of them are herding excited children. A few of the younger women help Mom prepare soup and sandwiches for later, while kids run around furniture and hide under tables playing games of tag and hide and seek. Two old women sit close together on the floor against the wall, wrapped in blankets. Their hollow eyes follow me as I get a plate of scrambled eggs and grab a piece of toast off a stack. I walk over and ask if I can get them anything, and they both shake their heads. They don't stop staring, and one finally asks in a raspy voice, "Yore one o'them, ain'tcha?"

I shrug as if I don't know what she's talking about. It seems our abilities are no secret in this community. I don't answer her. Sky comes through the pantry door carrying a pile of fresh blankets. She's wearing waders over her jeans and sweatshirt, and I remember Mom's admonition to wear rain gear.

"Where are all the men?" I ask Mom.

"They're where you and Sky are going; rescuing folks who wouldn't evacuate." I eat quickly and put my own waders on.

Pax? Jewel's voice is like sunshine in my brain. I'm at Storm's. Meet me here?

It makes sense to meet there because it's closer to the hollers, but I feel a cloud drift over the sun in my head. Storm.

We'll be there as soon as we can. Do you need us to bring anything?

Backpacks with supplies, water and food. You don't have a boat, do you? She's teasing. She knows we don't.

It takes longer to get there than we anticipated. Unrelenting rain makes it hard to see and high winds buffet the vehicle, pushing it from side to side. We maneuver around downed trees and avoid a section of road that was partially washed out. I wish I had Storm's ability right now.

The sheriff and a group of men are gathered around Sequoia's kitchen table, where a topographical map of the county lies pinned to a cork board. His radio squawks and after he listens to the report coming in, he removes a red map pin from one of the small valleys the locals call hollers, and pushes a blue one in. "Those folks are safely out of there."

He calls me over to the table. "Pax, can you and the girls get up to this area?" He points to a section near two creeks where six red pins indicate cabins that could be in trouble. I glance at the whole map and notice that there aren't that many red pins left, and they're spaced pretty widely apart. It looks like a few families might have banded into loose communities of sorts, but most of the mountain folk seem to prefer the isolation.

"Of course, Sheriff. We can use Jewel's and my cars, but what's the protocol for getting the people out of there?"

"Some of my men are already as close as they can get with rescue vehicles and equipment. We may need your tracking ability, Pax. The creeks are overflowing and the men report flash floods taking down some of the cabins."

"We're on our way."

Sky, you and Jewel ride together in her car. Follow me up the mountain. Storm, can you hear me?

I hear you. His voice is loud and clear. *Call me if you get stuck.* I imagine his amusement, but considering the conditions today, I might have to call him.

Where are you? I ask.

The sheriff told Wolf where you're going. I'm heading there now.

We make it to the staging area where a firetruck and ambulance are parked, and wait for Storm. He arrives a few minutes later, dressed in his riding rain gear and waders. He throws me a coil of rope and grabs another from the bed of his truck. *Men are already checking on the cabins on the other side of the creek. We'll take this side. Sky? Jewel? Are you okay with this?*

Of course we are, Jewel answers. *Let's get going.*

Sky says nothing, but I feel her raise up a wall of determination to cover a well of fear. I send out reassurance and she smiles.

The door of the first cabin we come to hangs by one hinge and swings back and forth as surging water ebbs and flows inside. It looks deserted, but if anyone is in there, Storm can get them out. "Is anybody here?" he shouts.

My sister reaches out with her feelers and shakes her head. I drop my guard and sniff. Under the scent of mold and rot, I smell old sweat and years of open-fire cooking baked into the exposed log walls. There's no fresh human scent. Storm contacts Wolf to report what we found, and we move on.

Jewel is becoming increasingly agitated. I feel Sky trying to calm her, but something is bothering her. I close my connection to the others and tap her number for a private conversation.

What's wrong, Jewel? She stumbles over an exposed root and I catch her arm to steady her.

It's the animals, Pax. I see their life-forces and some of them are so faint I know they're dying. I wonder how many people have drowned here today. How many are drowning right now?

She's ahead of me, but I see her back shaking as if she's sobbing. *I'm sorry, honey.* Did I really just call her honey? I hope she didn't catch that.

I continue trying to reassure her. *Most of the people who can are out searching. No drownings have been reported so far, and it's possible that no one lost their life today. I wish we could help with the animals, too.*

"Over there," Storm says, pointing to a darker shadow in the forest. I break connection with Jewel and rejoin the group link. Half of the roof of the dilapidated cabin has caved in. It looks like it's been uninhabited for a long time. We enter and look around. Sky again sends out feelers, I sniff and Jewel walks around outside to see if anyone might be hurt out there, but it's empty of life. Storm reports in and we slowly make our way up steep ground, treacherous with mud and wet leaves.

The third cabin is close to the creek, now more like a gushing river full of debris from the hills. From here it looks like water is halfway up to the windows. It creaks and groans and I wonder how long it'll be able to stand against the raging current.

"Is anyone home?" Storm shouts.

This time there's an answering shout, "In here. We need help!"

The thought comes from Jewel. *That sounds like Marla.*

Sky nods and says out loud, "It is, and someone's with her." I drop my coil of rope, tie it around my waist and hand it to Storm. He wraps a coil around his own waist and ties the rest to a solid-looking oak. "You girls get ready. I hope you brought survival blankets."

Of course we did, Jewel answers. *Get them out of there before the water washes the cabin downstream.*

When we're ten feet from the cabin we hear a loud crash followed by screams. The logs shudder and shift and a section of roof falls in. Part of the log wall closest to the creek breaks off and I know it's only a matter of seconds before the whole thing washes away with two people inside. We're out of time.

"Storm!" I shout. I can barely hear his answer, muffled by the roar of the wild creek. The rest of the roof peels away.

Tell Marla to hold on to the other person in there. His mental shout hurts, but I do as he says and yell his instructions as loudly as I can. A moment later, she floats out of the roofless house holding tightly to someone wrapped in a blanket. As soon as they clear the cabin, it groans loudly and splinters as the torrent sweeps it away.

Storm sets them down in front of the girls. Jewel wraps a lightweight survival blanket around Marla's shoulders and gently pulls her from the person she's gripping. Sky pulls the soggy blanket away to reveal Marla's mother, pale and unconscious. She tosses the wet blanket aside and wraps her in a second survival blanket.

"This is the last of them on this side," Storm says. "Let's get them back to the staging area." He lifts the unconscious woman a couple of feet from the forest floor as if she's on a gurney, and Marla stumbles along, occasionally touching her mother's head. We slip and slide down the mountain to the waiting ambulance and trucks.

As soon as she sees her mother safely in the ambulance she turns to us and says, "I owe you one," and climbs in beside her. The driver tells Storm they're heading to the Adams' house where a triage center has been set up. All the roads to area hospitals are impassable, but a helicopter can land in their field if necessary, as soon as the weather clears.

Wild Bill Stern approaches us as we watch the ambulance pull away. "We're splitting you up. Sky, you'll go with Rob Townsend and his group. Jewel, you're with Dan Jones's group, Storm is with Hunter Smith and you're with me, Pax."

The men Bill mentions are members of the tribal council. Rob is the pharmacist and leader of the Paint Clan. Dan owns Blue Mountain Construction and leads the Blue Clan. Hunter runs the hunting shop and heads up the mixed martial arts dojo where Storm trains. He's the leader of the Deer Clan. Bill Stern heads up the Wild Potato Clan. I think it's fitting that he owns the grocery store.

I tap my wristband. *Let's keep the link open. We can keep our folks informed, too.* Everyone agrees and we follow our groups to the vehicles. I ride with Wild Bill in his enormous truck with oversized tires.

"We're going downriver. If anyone got swept up in the flood, that's where we'll find them. Pray we find living survivors." I send up a quick prayer. I am not looking forward to this.

We don't speak any more until we get to the staging area where we split up into teams. Some teams head farther upstream and Bill and I go downstream toward a swirling morass where two creeks have overflowed and run into each other. Broken trees and the splintered remains of cabins mixed with oil and trash, shift and eddy in the current. It's impossible to see into the muddy mess.

I let my scent guard down, sniff and immediately wish I hadn't. Nothing is worse than the smell of a corpse; even a recently deceased one. I follow my nose and point to a bank where I spot a pale hand sticking up through the mud. It's no wonder cadaver dogs get depressed.

Bill uses a trowel to dig around the body until he finds the face. The way his mouth turns down and his eyes grow sad it's obvious that it's someone he knows. He calls it in and marks the spot next to the body with a circle of bright yellow spray paint.

We move farther downstream and I sniff the air, hoping to get a whiff of someone alive. I find a boy and girl hugging each other and shivering on a tiny island near solid ground, but not close enough for them to cross. He looks to be about ten and she's even younger.

"Where are your folks?" Bill shouts. The boy shrugs and shakes his head. They must have been separated. I hope the body we found isn't their father.

I wrap a rope around my waist and Bill ties the other end to the tree. *Thanks, Mom, for making me wear my waders.*

I'll let her know you said that, Sky answers.

I nearly trip and fall into the sludge, but manage to push through. The little girl climbs up on my back, wraps her legs around my waist and her arms a little too tightly around my throat. Her brother's eyes are so wide with fear I'm afraid they might pop out of his head. He nods when I tell him to wait. "I'll be right back for you. I promise."

It takes several minutes to fight my way back to shore where I hand the girl over to Bill. He quickly wraps her in a survival blanket. By the time I get back to the island, her brother is shivering so much I'm afraid his teeth will shatter. He manages to climb onto my back and hold on long enough for me to get him to safety. Instead of taking the blanket Bill offers him, he snuggles in with his sister. Bill calls for a backup team on his radio and we wait. I sit next to the kids and pull them into a hug. After a while, their shivering slows and they greedily accept the water and granola bars Bill hands them.

A deputy comes to get us, driving Bill's truck. The giant tires give it better traction than the police SUVs. I climb into the back seat with the kids and Bill turns up the heat. Then he and the deputy go dig out the body, lay it in the bed and cover it with a tarp.

By the end of the day, six bodies have been found, eighteen people are still missing, and dozens of families are homeless. Every muscle in my body aches; especially my heart.

FORTY

JEWEL

"Lady, I'm hungwy," a child's voice drags me out of a dreamless sleep. Child? I sit up and nearly fall out of the narrow cot I'm in and wish I could stuff the sudden memories back into the dark. Floods, pain, blood, broken bones, cracked heads, fading auras and dying animals; it's all too much and my eyes fill with tears. I feel a tug on the blanket and stare into the face of a little girl no more than three years old, with pleading eyes and a thumb in her mouth. I wipe my hands over my face, stand up and remember that I went to bed fully clothed so as not to waste time this morning. Sky did the same. She's asleep in the cot next to mine. On the other side of Dad's office, the boys' cots are empty. They were asleep when I tumbled into mine last night. They must have left before daybreak this morning. Six more cots are lined up in the spacious office; most of them empty but obviously slept in.

"Come on, sweetie. Let's get you some breakfast." We go upstairs to the kitchen and I turn her over to her mom who's busy scrambling eggs. All of the furniture is pushed against the walls to leave room for cots in the middle. Our house has been turned into a triage and treatment center until the injured can be taken to area hospitals. The medical experts who were able to get here, including Sequoia, are staying in my bedroom and the guest rooms. Mom didn't want to separate families, so the children of many of the injured are here, too. Some of the kids are also in need of medical treatment.

Dylan and Coral have opened their home to the folks who aren't injured or sick. I wish they all had access to the alien tech that protects our houses, but it might not have prevented them from being washed off the mountain.

Sequoia and a couple of doctors are talking quietly to patients. I recognize Miss Allen, our school nurse. Both Pastor John and Pastor Mike are here. I spot Marla asleep on the couch next to the cot holding Mrs. Snow. Her reptilian appearance disturbs me, so I grab a cup of coffee and go back downstairs to wake up Sky. Mom follows me down.

"We need you girls here today," she says while Sky stretches and sits up with a yawn. "Until the weather clears and helicopters can safely land, we're the hospital. We have basic medical supplies, but we'll need you to tell us who's most critical and where they're hurt. We expect that more people will be coming in today."

By the time we return upstairs, Marla is up, holding a plate of food on her lap. I watch her help her mother sit up and offer her something to drink. I tap my wristband for Sky and when I get her attention, I nod toward Marla.

She's no different than we are. We're hybrids, too. I think we should try to be her friends.

The difference is, she's part Dracan and we're part Allaran. How do we know what abilities she has? I don't know if we can trust her. Sky is frowning, and I'm afraid she's right.

Let's give her a chance. She did say she owes us one. I don't mention that her weak aura, scaly skin, and sharp teeth give me the creeps. I'm determined to get over it, knowing I'm the only one who can see her as she is.

Sky breaks the connection and a second later opens the link with all of us. *Pax, where are you? Is Storm with you?*

Storm's with Wolf and another team and I'm back with Wild Bill. We've found a few more survivors. The ambulance is headed your way.

Have you found any more bodies? I ask.

No, Jewel, and I sincerely hope we don't.

Same here, Buddy, Storm chimes in. *Wolf and I are combing some of the most remote locations beyond the Dome. Haven't found anyone yet, but we'll keep looking until we're reasonably sure it's clear up here. You girls stay out of trouble in that nice dry house. If the rain doesn't stop soon, we might need gills.*

I laugh and walk over to Sequoia. "What do you need me to do?" I ask.

The morning flies by in a blur as we tend to the injured. New people come in waves as the ambulances drop them off. Sky and I team up and go from bed to bed. She picks up pain signals projected by the patients, and I find where the injury is by spots in their energy field, which appear to be muddied versions of their natural aura colors. I soon realize that the mustard-yellow streaks mark places where bones are broken.

I find a patient with a severely faded aura over an injury. The doctor looks worried as he uncovers the wound. It looks infected and I turn away, feeling sick to my stomach. Sky sends reassurance my way until I feel better.

Marla helps the doctors by fetching bandages, splints and supplies. She knows a few of the patients and stops to encourage them. This is a side of her I've never seen, and I'm beginning to think we can actually be friends.

Mom and the ladies have prepared soup and sandwiches for lunch and laid it out on the breakfast counter cafeteria-style. Sky and I get lunch for those who can't stand in line. Once everyone has been fed, we get our own lunches and take our plates downstairs for a break. Marla follows us.

Be nice to Marla, I tell Sky. *She's been really caring and helpful today.*

I'll try. I notice she isn't saying anything out loud, which isn't like her.

"How's your mom?" I ask Marla.

"Why? What do you care?" she snaps, her voice as sharp as always.

Sky rolls her eyes at me. *See what I mean? She is not our friend and doesn't want to be.*

It takes me a second to rein in my temper, but I know that if I were in Marla's place, watching over my injured mother, I might be irritable too. I turn to Marla and say, "What makes you think I don't care?"

Then Marla does the unthinkable. She apologizes. "I'm sorry, Jewel. I don't know what's gotten into me, but it isn't fair to you. You did save our lives, after all."

Sky and I look at each other in disbelief, but I quickly recover.

"No problem. We're all under a lot of stress. I'll be glad when this is over."

~~~~~

Throughout the afternoon, ambulances bring more injured people to us. Mom and her helpers are kept busy preparing food for the crowd. Some of the new arrivals are starving and get a bowl of nourishing soup right away. Supper is cooking in a row of crock-pots, and once again, I'm thankful for the Cherokee women.

The boys come in after dark, dragging their feet, slouched over with fatigue. They both have muddy auras and I rush to them, concerned that they're hurt.

Their pain is on the inside, Sky assures me. *They're hungry but not injured.* We haven't heard from them since this morning, but when I ask for an update, they both shake their heads.

Not now, Jewel. Pax's thoughts sound tired. Sky reaches for his hand. *We need to get cleaned up and eat first.*

Marla helps us get supper to the bedridden patients while the boys hit the showers. The front door has been opening all day and we barely notice when Sheriff Green and Max walk in. They shake the water off their jackets and remove their boots. The sheriff is warmly welcomed and Mom fixes a plate for him.

Max spots Marla on the couch with a tray of food on her lap helping her mother eat. "Hey, girl," he shouts. She shushes him and he ignores her warning. "Have you been here all day?"

Sequoia rushes over to him and says something too quietly for me to hear. He looks like he's about to argue with her and then thinks better of it. Instead, he turns to Marla and speaks more quietly. She has a disgusted look on her face. I wonder what she sees in him.

He suddenly grabs her hand and pulls her to her feet. She drops the food tray and yanks herself away from him.

"Leave me alone!" she hisses. Everyone in the room turns to stare at them.

Storm and Pax must have come in while our attention was on the drama. They make their way through the rows of cots, and Pax gets down to pick up the dishes and splattered food. He doesn't say anything. Storm, on the other hand, has plenty to say.

"Max, if you can't behave like a human being, then please leave."

"You're one to talk about humans, Storm," Max replies. "You and your hybrid friends...." His words end abruptly and he covers his throat with his hands. His feet rise several inches off the floor, but Storm isn't touching him. His face turns red, but I see that he's breathing. I'm surprised Sheriff Green hasn't interfered yet, and by the look on Max's face, so is he.

"You know what I'm capable of." Storm's steely look belies his quiet, steady voice. "When I release you, put on your jacket and walk out of here." At that, he lets him go.

"I'm going to get something to eat," Max says, still defiant.

"Not here," Storm replies.

An ambulance driver who's finished eating offers to take Max to the Fletchers. Sheriff Green nods at his son and indicates he should go with him. Before he leaves, Max glares first at Marla and then at Storm. "This isn't finished."

I bring a fresh tray of food over to Marla, who looks angry enough to throw it. Her aura momentarily brightens, and I realize her reptilian appearance no longer revolts me.

I can't see her like you can, but I'm starting to like her, Sky says in my head. I wonder if I projected my thoughts, or is she getting better at reading them?

Storm helps Mom and the ladies clean up after supper. I can see the exhaustion on my mother's face and her aura has lost some of its brightness. I hope she and the ladies get some sleep tonight.

The four of us invite Marla to join us in the office to watch the news. We're hoping for some good news, of course, but lately everything has been about terrible weather and disasters around the country. Still, it's better to know what's coming than to be ignorant of danger. The children who share our room are already asleep and we keep the volume on the television low.

*****

Breaking News: "Sustained winds of 45 miles per hour and heavy rains hampered rescue efforts throughout the Great Smoky Mountains today. Countless cabins were washed away by flooding and at least fifteen people have been reported dead so far. The number of casualties is expected to rise as rescue efforts continue."

"The mountain slide in Blue Mountain combined with adverse weather conditions has cut the area off from surrounding hospitals. We're getting reports in from law enforcement that several homes are being used as shelters and first aid centers. Roads are too badly damaged to allow rescue vehicles in from the outside, and all choppers are grounded until the weather clears, including our own news helicopters.

"The storm system is expected to move out early tomorrow morning. We expect clear skies and calm winds tomorrow. The change in weather should help the rescue efforts. We'll keep you updated. - Kyle Johnson, reporting for Cherokee Nation News."

*****

Sky, Storm, and Pax are asleep before the news is over and I turn off the TV. Marla goes back upstairs to be with her mother and I lie down, thinking my mind is too busy to sleep. I'm wrong.

FORTY-ONE

The boys are once again gone when I wake up, but Sky is still asleep. When I get to the kitchen, the sunlight streaming in through our enormous windows is a happy surprise. The thwop-thwop of helicopter blades sounds like heaven to my ears. Soon paramedics are loading the most seriously injured people onto gurneys for their ride to a real hospital.

More patients are up and able to get their own breakfast, and even those who can't and are conscious have smiles on their faces. It is such a relief that the storm is finally over.

I step out on the porch and see several news choppers hovering over the woods. Two of the Sentinels gleam high above them, mine and Sky's. A chopper warms up and takes off from the field in front of our house. This one carries Marla and her mother.

Sky comes outside holding two cups of coffee, and hands me one.

"I've been thinking," I say to her. "Do you remember the symbols on and around the tetrahedron on Sequoia's blanket?"

"Sure, I remember," she answers. "What about them?"

"It doesn't look like we'll be busy here today. I'll grab my laptop from my room and we can find a quiet place to look them up online. I'd love to know what they mean."

"Can't we just ask her?"

"She's not here right now. We might need to know what they mean when we find the artifact, and there's no telling when Sequoia will have time to explain them to us, or if she even can."

"Let's do it." Sky nods and we head to my room. I knock on the door and enter when I hear no answer. The laptop is in its case on the floor of the closet. I don't disturb any of our guests' items and we quickly retreat to the hallway and close the door.

"Where to?" she asks.

"Mom and Dad's room. I don't mind if they come in, but I'd rather not let anyone else know what we're looking for."

"Do you remember what they were?"

"I have a pretty good recall of shapes. Let's start by looking up Cherokee symbols and see if we recognize any." We plop down on my parents' bed and open the laptop.

Sky? Jewel? Pax calls over our link. *Where are you?*

We're in my parents' room. I answer. *Where are you?*

Storm and I are coming back. They're calling off the searches. It feels like we've covered every square inch of the county and there are no more cabins to search. The choppers will be able to see more from the air.

It's a good thing we're sparsely populated up here, Storm breaks in. *I'm looking forward to a hot shower and a little downtime.*

I don't tell them how glad I am that they're coming home, but Sky shoots me a look and smiles. I know she feels the same.

Our search brings up some of the symbols I recognize, but the overall patterns are different. If I remember correctly, in the middle of the tetrahedron is a circle with a cross in the center, cutting it into four equal sections. One website says it depicts the four seasons, another says it's the four directions and yet another claims it represents fire, air, water and earth.

"I remember figures in each of the quadrants, two males and two females."

"That obviously represents us," Sky points out. "Wasn't there something else around it? I wish I had taken a snapshot."

"I did," Pax says from the doorway. He comes in and Storm follows him. "We heard what you said about the figures in the circle. Let me find that photo." He searches his phone and shows us what the blanket looks like. He sits on the bed next to me and Storm plops down next to Sky.

"I've memorized the symbols," Storm says, "and I know what most of them probably mean. The combinations are open for interpretation, but we know a few things and might be able to figure out the rest. We know the stick figures represent us, for example, and we'll call the circle we're in the earth circle."

A smaller ring with short nubby spokes extending from it sits above the earth circle, and a dark, narrow horizontal half-moon forms a shallow bowl that cradles it on the bottom.

"Those two symbols together, without the one in the middle, represent love," Sky says, "so can we assume that love plays a part in saving the artifact? But what does that mean, exactly? How?"

"Look at this, on the left of the tetrahedron," Pax points to the photo on his phone. "There's a vertical half-moon, and underneath it an arrow pointing to the artifact. What about the winged serpent below the arrow? What do those symbols mean?"

Storm answers, "The moon is the protector and guardian of the earth. See the feathered wings on the serpent? It's an ambivalent symbol, and could either mean an evil entity or a scary one with good intentions. If we consider the moon represents the Allarans, the serpent would be the Dracans. We already know that some are working with the Allarans to protect the artifact."

"What does the arrow mean?" asks Sky.

"Arrows typically signify protection and defense," Storm says.

"So this symbol might mean that the Allarans will defend the artifact against the Dracans, or that they'll defend it together. But from what?" Pax asks.

"What about this symbol on the right of the tetrahedron?" I point to the photo. "It looks like a stylized dog with big ears next to a four-pointed star, which is next to a butterfly. Do you know what they mean, Storm?"

"The dog-like creature is a coyote, or trickster. The star represents courage, hope and guidance, and the butterfly means transformation. I'm not sure how they fit together. Maybe it's one of those things we can't interpret before the right time. I can tell you what the eight-pointed sun in the circle at the bottom of the artifact represents. It's hope."

"Where there's life, there's hope," says Sky. "Isn't that in the Bible or something?"

"Now the question is when? Do you think we'll be ready?" I feel anxiety rising. Waiting is not easy.

"Speaking of getting ready, I need a shower and some lunch. I'll see you girls later." Storm gets up and leaves.

I hand Pax's phone back to him, and feel a little jolt where my hand momentarily touches his. I glance at him and smile, but fight the urge to stare at his emerald eyes. They pull me like a pair of powerful magnets, and if I give in, he'll know I'm attracted to him as more than a friend. There's too much at stake for complicated romantic entanglements. It's best to keep things light and easy between us.

"Brother, dear," Sky says sweetly, "I don't have your gift, but even I can tell you need a shower, too. Now go."

He reaches over me and pats her on the head. "See you at lunch, kiddo."

FORTY-TWO

Wolf, Dylan, and a few others have gone to the twins' house, and Dad and the rest of the rescue workers are here for lunch and a much-needed break. They're folding the empty cots and carrying them downstairs. After cleaning up, Storm and Pax move furniture back in place. Cots are left ready in the office for people who have no other shelter, and I see quite a few women and kids still here among the men. Mom has sandwiches and soup ready, and we take our plates outside.

Sky and I sit on the porch swing while the boys take a couple of chairs next to a small table. I'm happy to see critters busy in the field and our four Sentinels floating placidly in the sky. Life seems to have returned to normal. We eat in silence, enjoying the peace.

Storm is the first to break it. "Did any of you ever find out what Marla's mom was doing in the Dracan tunnels?"

"She was hurt, Storm, and we were pretty busy," Sky answers. "There was no opportunity to question her. Besides, Marla stayed pretty close to her until they were evacuated this morning."

"How did it go with Marla?" Pax asks.

I shrug my shoulders and answer, "Not badly. It occurred to me that we're all hybrids, and maybe we can be friends, or at least tolerate each other. Marla showed a lot of compassion while she cared for the sick and injured. She surprised me."

Sky continues, "She even apologized for snapping at Jewel. If she can stay away from Max, there's hope for her."

I see a sudden flurry of activity among the field animals and hundreds of birds take to the air from the forest and fly scattered and confused away from the trees. It looks like every bird for himself. What now?

The sound starts as a deep rumble I feel in my gut before it reaches my ears. When it does, I drop to the floor and cover my head, and scream, "Get down! Cover your ears!"

The volume increases and wave after wave of vibrations beat against me and bounce off the wall behind me, hitting me again from that side. Screaming pain rips at my ears and head. It feels like muscle and sinew are tearing apart as it travels through every cell in my body. My heart slams against my chest and I know I'm going to die.

After an eternity, I feel the vibrations lessen and finally stop. There is no sound at all, and I'm sure this time I've been deafened forever. I tap my wrist.

Sky? Storm? Pax? I hope I can still hear their thoughts. Nothing.

Sky is curled up a couple of feet away. I crawl over and shake her. She squirms, so I know she's alive. I stagger to my feet and shuffle over to Pax. His eyes are open and staring at the ceiling, and I feel my heart turn to ice. Is he dead? No. His eyes find me and track me as I step over him. Storm is on his side facing away from me. I roll him over and he blinks. We're alive, but in what condition?

The door opens behind us and I feel Dad's strong arms pull me toward him. He leads me inside while other men help my friends. Mom is speaking but I can't hear a word she says. Dad helps me sit in my reading chair. Pax and Sky are led to the couch, and Storm walks to the other recliner.

Whoever said "silence is golden" has never heard silence like this. It feels heavy, confining, as if my head were filled with cement. It gradually lightens, while Mom and the ladies fuss over us. I tap on the wristband again.

It's too quiet in here. Will someone please answer me?

Oh, thank God our link still works. Sky bursts into tears, and Mom goes to her and hugs her. I tap "M" and she looks at me.

We can still communicate, Mom. We'll be okay, even if this is permanent. It's the first time I've admitted my fear to myself. What if we never hear again?

We're all having trouble hearing, Jewel, she answers. *You were outside, so it's worse for you kids, but I'm getting some hearing back and trust that you'll recover, too. You did the last time this happened.*

I nod. I'm willing to hope, but the last time wasn't nearly as bad. Is this it? Is this our call?

I end the connection with Mom and link with the kids again.

Do you think the artifact just called us? Storm and I must be on the same wavelength because that's exactly what I'm thinking.

We'll know soon enough, Pax says. *We'll be hearing from the Watchers if it's time. I don't know about you guys, but I'm wiped out and think I'll take advantage of this forced quiet.* He presses on the band and cuts the link, curls up with his head on the arm of the sofa and closes his eyes.

Sky lies down on the other side and cuts her link. Storm and I do the same and curl up in our recliners. I'm drifting off when I feel a warm blanket cover me. Mom.

FORTY-THREE

PAX

I swat at the flies buzzing around my head. The noise only becomes louder, I come fully awake and realize I'm hearing sound again. Nothing is clear yet, but I'm hopeful it will clear up eventually. Meanwhile, we have our telepathy to fall back on. I smile and then open my eyes.

Jewel is still asleep, her face cradled on her hand. Some of her jet-black hair cascades along her soft cheek and down her neck. I love how her lashes brush her cheek, and imagine her long legs tucked under the blanket. Rein it in. Just friends, remember?

There's that buzzing again. It feels almost like it did when the Watchers communicated with us.

If you are awake, please awaken the others. You must come right away.

Oh, no. It is the Watchers.

Give us some time to get ready. Where should we meet you? I answer.

Sequoia comes to you. She will lead you. You must come now, Paxton. It is time.

My stomach drops and I feel sick. We aren't ready. What if we can't do what is being asked of us? What if we fail? I push the thoughts aside and get up to shake Storm awake. He's groggy, but I see his eyes go wide and know he's hearing them, too.

Sky sits up and sends a wave of fear and confusion. I send her peace and go to Jewel. I gently brush her hair away from her face. It's as soft as I've imagined it to be. I shake her shoulder until her eyes open.

"I hear them, Pax," she says. Her voice is slightly roughened by sleep, and I feel my body respond. I turn away as she sits up. At least I'm hearing clearer.

Analiese sets a tray of coffee, mugs, and biscuits on the table. My stomach rumbles and my mouth waters in response. "How long have we slept?" I ask her.

She smiles, pours a cup that smells like heaven, and says, as she hands it to me, "You slept all night. It's nearly 10 a.m. Wednesday."

Jewel's house has many bathrooms and we each find one and freshen up. The girls, as usual, take longer than Storm and me. Sequoia and Wolf come in the front door and head into the kitchen. Mom and Dad arrive soon after, and they gather in the living room with Analiese and Charles.

"The Watchers have called the kids," Wolf explains. "They'll allow us to accompany them to a place below the observatory on Clingman's Dome. Sequoia and I have packed supplies for them, including headlamps, flashlights, rope, batteries, water and food. The Watcher's say they won't need it all, but they will allow them to carry the backpacks. The only thing left for us to do is pray for them."

The adults clasp hands and bow their heads. Wolf leads them in a prayer for our protection and for wisdom to know what to do when the time comes. I silently pray along. I pray that God cares enough to listen and answer our prayers.

I see Storm standing silently at the kitchen counter. The look on his face matches his name. I can smell his anger.

When the girls return, we grab our jackets, put on hiking boots, and get in our separate cars. Sky and I ride with our parents, Jewel with hers, and Storm with his aunt and uncle. If things go badly, this may be the last time we get to spend with our families.

Wolf and Sequoia lead us to a clearing where the three cars park in a row, and we walk along a narrow path that winds through the forest and up a steep incline. On the way up, we get glimpses of mountain views obscured by the blue haze that gives the Great Smoky Mountains their name. The Watchers wait in front of a wall of brambles in a small clearing.

The Watcher in the middle steps forward. *We enter the mountain here. Only the Four are permitted inside the chamber of the artifact. You must take your leave now, Star Children, and follow us.*

Mom and Dad gather Sky and me into a hug, and then hug Storm and Jewel, too. The other folks do the same, giving each of us encouragement and assuring us they'll be waiting when we return.

Then it's time, and the middle Watcher aims a beam from a device he holds in one hand at the brambles. The plants disappear to reveal an opening large enough to walk upright and alongside each other. As we enter a corridor with smooth, straight walls, I look back and see the brambles move back into place.

"This looks like one of the Dracan tunnels," Storm observes. "Is it?"

No, Star Child. We also form tunnels in the earth, but our technology is different. I notice they seem to be floating, and they emit a glow that provides enough light that we don't need to turn our headlamps on. It's as if we're following ghosts.

"What are the chances we'll run into some of the Dracans down here?" Sky asks. No one answers. She isn't projecting any anxiety, but I feel her presence as a constant, warm energy. I drop my shield and sniff. She and Jewel are ahead of me and Storm walks in front of them. Jewel's scent fills me with a longing I have never felt before. Sky's scent is as familiar as my own, and Storm is sending out anger pheromones, a little stronger than usual. It's evident that our gifts work in these Allaran tunnels. The Dracans must use something that coats theirs and dampens our abilities.

The tunnel angles downward for about thirty yards until it branches and we follow the Watchers down the left branch. The walls close in so that we're forced to walk single-file. They lead us along another branch to the right, and then another, until I've lost count of the turns. We'd never find our way back without them.

After what seems like hours, we reach a staircase cut into the stone walls of a square shaft. Each flight has twelve steps to a landing, where it turns to follow the next wall down twelve steps to the next landing, and so on. I look down but see only darkness after several flights below. The little men start down the stairs without changing pace and I see that they actually are floating. I tap my wristband.

Are you floating them, Storm?

Not me. I'm guessing they're doing it on their own.

The now familiar buzzing tells me one of the Watchers is speaking. *We have many abilities, young Paxton. We are born from the same source as you.* It seems they heard our mental conversation and can tap in to our link.

Then why do you need us to fix the artifact? Jewel breaks in. *If you have the same gifts, can't you fix it?*

The question seems to stump the Watchers because they don't answer. I try to count the flights of stairs but by the time I get to sixty, my leg muscles are quivering and my mind has gone blank.

"Don't you believe in elevators?" Storm asks irritably.

We will stop here and you may rest a bit.

We gratefully sink to a step and grab a bottle of water from our packs. Sky offers water to the Watchers but they shake their heads. I wonder if they eat and drink. They gather closely together and I imagine they're communicating with each other. It seems a good time to study them.

Their bald heads are shaped like giant light bulbs held to thin bodies by a short stick of a neck. Eyes, shaped like ours but much larger with solid black irises, dominate their faces. In comparison, their noses and thin mouths look disproportionately small. I look for distinguishing features and can't find anything that gives them individual identities, although I'm sure they can tell each other apart. Are they triplets?

One of them floats over to us. *You asked why we cannot fix the artifact if we share the same abilities you have. We cannot, Star Children, because we lack your human genes. You are of Terra and we are not. Your planet, created for you, responds to you. Although we have been here for many millennia, we were created for Allara, as were the Allarans, and the Dracans were created for their planet. You have been chosen and you alone can complete the task. If you are sufficiently refreshed, we will proceed.*

We gather our things and pull ourselves to our feet. I hear Jewel groan and Sky stretches her legs. I look up and can't see where we entered this endless stairwell. I don't bother looking down again. We're certainly going to feel this tomorrow; if there is a tomorrow.

Although I've lost count of the number of landings we've passed this far, I start over from our rest stop. It helps to pass the time and keeps my mind off my sore legs. When I've counted twenty-nine more flights, I feel the step under my feet tremble. It quickly turns into violent shaking and a roar fills the shaft.

"Stop!" I yell. "Hug the wall!" I grab Jewel just ahead of me and turn us both to the wall.

"I have Sky," Storm yells. The Watchers say nothing, and I hope they're holding on to something.

My face is turned so I can see stones and broken stairs fall from high above, bouncing off and breaking the stairs below them as they tumble down.

A violent shudder knocks me free of the wall, and I hear Jewel scream my name as my feet slip off the step and I'm suddenly in free fall. I'm dead. I close my eyes, knowing it's over, when I feel the whoosh of a chunk of rock shooting past me. Storm. Thank God for Storm. He floats me to the side, and my foot finds a solid step, but my legs refuse to hold me up and I abruptly sit.

When the shaking stops, the stairs are all but obliterated. Jewel and Sky are shaking and holding on to each other, and I send as much peace as I can muster to my sister. Storm makes his way down to me and sits on a relatively intact step above me. The Watchers are gathered on a landing that seems to have escaped major damage. Now what?

~~~~~

It's a miracle we each still have our backpacks. I take mine off and grab a water bottle.

What do we do now? Jewel asks. Her thoughts sound as shaky as I feel.

We wait for the Watchers, Storm answers. *It looks like they're having a little conference.*

We don't have to wait long. *We continue, Star Children. The Dracans are drilling closer than we expected. We must get to the artifact before they find it.*

How to you propose we do that, with the stairs destroyed? I ask. As far as I can see, ours is the only section still intact.

If we hang on to each other, Storm says, *I can float us down, as long as it isn't too far.*

How far is too far? Jewel asks.

A Watcher answers. *We are close. My brothers and I will help you, Storm.*

We hold hands in a circle and the Watchers gather around us. It feels like a platform is under our feet as we float out into the middle of the shaft and begin to drop. I close my eyes and pretend we're in an elevator. Why didn't we do this from the beginning? It would have saved time and muscle pain.

Rocks and broken stairs cover the bottom of the shaft. The Watchers lead us to a narrow opening, where Storm tosses aside the debris blocking it. We enter another tunnel, with walls that look melted, like cooled lava, and a floor and ceiling that curve around us. Is this an ancient lava tube? We follow them for what seem like miles. Sky stumbles and I call a halt.

"We need to stop and eat something." My voice is strangely muffled. I'm not claustrophobic, but the thought of tons of rock above us makes me uncomfortable. Another shaking could bring the mountain down on top of us. And how are we getting oxygen this far down?

Patience; we will stop soon, Star Children. There is a place just ahead.

FORTY-FOUR

The Watchers lead us to a room about fifteen feet square filled with natural light that comes from openings near the top edge of the walls on all four sides. A closed wooden door takes up nearly all of one wall. Stone benches covered with soft cushions line the walls to our right and left. Tables topped with ornate mosaics of swirling colors sit in front of the benches. Jewel will love these.

A large mosaic of Earth, covered by the mesh of the power grid adorns the right wall and another, this one of Earth with the outline of a tetrahedron enclosing it, is on the left.

I smell fresh forest air, redolent with the unique autumn scent of damp leaves and fungus. It feels as if we're on or near the surface.

"How deep are we?" I ask. "All those stairs certainly weren't an illusion. We can't be near the surface, can we?"

No, young Paxton. We are deep in the heart of the mountain.

"Then is the air and light an illusion?" Storm is as curious as I am.

Both air and light are brought in using Allaran technology. The openings on the surface are undetectable by most humans and Dracans.

Sky and Jewel set their backpacks on a bench and take out sandwiches and water, and we greedily tear into the food. Jewel's eyes sparkle in the light as I watch her take in the beautiful colors of the mosaics. I feel Sky's joy, and even Storm seems more relaxed.

When we're finished, the large door swings open and the Watchers lead us into a wide corridor lined with arched doors on both sides. This may be their living quarters. More colorful designs cover the walls. I'm amazed that I no longer sense the weight of the mountain above us; at least not until a sudden loud bang reverberates through the hall and I feel vibrations through my boots.

I hear a sizzling sound and the vibrations increase.

We must hurry, a Watcher says and the buzzing that accompanies their mind-speech grows louder and more urgent.

We run down the long corridor to a solid metal door at the end. It opens as we near it, and slams shut with a bang behind us, leaving the Watchers on the other side, still in the corridor.

Storm and I turn to open the door for them, but there's no handle and it's sealed shut. I see his face twist in concentration and know he's trying to move it telekinetically. It doesn't budge. We're trapped.

"There's nothing we can do, we have to find the artifact," Storm says.

"Wait! Maybe they'll follow us once they've taken care of whatever that noise was." Jewel suggests. Sky nods enthusiastically.

"What if they can't?" Storm snaps. I find myself agreeing with him. We'd heard a similar sizzling when we encountered the Dracans digging under Hunter's woods. If the Watchers are fighting the Dracans, my bet would be on the Dracans to win.

"Right now the artifact is the main thing. If we don't find it and fix it, our whole planet will die." I turn away from the door, which is outlined on this side by pale light. Ahead of us is complete darkness, and I'm grateful that Wolf and Sequoia packed flashlights and miner hats. I adjust my backpack and turn on my headlamp. "Let's go."

I take the lead, Storm the rear and the girls walk single-file between us. Our lights reveal the uneven damp walls of a natural tunnel uninterrupted by cross tunnels. We have no choice but to move forward, and I'm grateful. It's bad enough that we've been abandoned here. It would be a lot worse if we got ourselves lost in a maze.

I drop my scent shield and sniff the air. I smell a freshening ahead of us, coming from a much larger space. After a few minutes, we come to a cavern large enough to swallow all but a small circle of light around us. Do we follow the wall to our left or to our right? I tap on my wristband.

Straight ahead? Right? Left? What do you think?

Sky answers. *Do you smell anything unusual that might guide us, Pax?*

It smells like a big cave, but if the artifact has a unique scent, I'm not getting it.

I see something alive glowing to the right. Maybe we should check it out, Jewel breaks in.

Let's head that way, says Storm. *We can always follow the wall back if there's nothing there.*

We follow the right wall along a wide ledge that narrows in places where it's crumbled away. We pass some paths that angle down into the cavern, but feel more secure hugging the wall. I step aside to let Jewel lead the way when we get closer to the glowing thing she still sees.

When she spots it, she shines her headlamp on it so we can see it, too. A centipede at least ten inches long clings to the rock wall. I hear Sky's thought. *Yuck.*

There aren't too many animals that can live in deep caves, Jewel explains. *I was hoping we'd find more and they could help light a path, but that isn't going to happen.*

I hear water trickling deeper in the cavern, Storm says. *I've heard there are fish and salamanders in caves. Do you think you'd be able to see them, Jewel?*

If they're alive, I can see them. We're getting nowhere here. Is anybody else ready to head into the cave?

Storm puts his backpack down and pulls out a looped rope. He ties one end around his waist, plays out about five feet and holds it out to Sky. She does the same and hands the next length to Jewel.

Jewel hands it to me without tying up. *Since I can see living creatures, shouldn't I take the lead?*

The others agree, so I reluctantly take the loop, tie it and hand the rest to Jewel, who ties the remaining rope around her makeshift belt. I don't like the idea of Jewel being the first. What if something happens to her? What if she trips or, worse, falls down a crevasse? What if I lose her?

The girls shrug into their backpacks and Jewel leads us back the way we came. I send up a silent prayer.

FORTY-FIVE

JEWEL

It makes sense to go back to the place where we entered the cave. I find the path that leads directly into the cavern from the entrance, and we follow it downward toward the sound of water. The light from my headlamp illuminates the path only a few feet in front of me, and I quickly lose track of how far we've come.

A stream appears from the left and runs parallel to the trail. I see the glow of fish and some animals that look like elongated crawfish swimming in the water. I wonder how they manage to live with no light. What do they eat? I shine my headlamp on one rather large fish, but the light reflects off the black water, concealing it from the others' view.

We follow the stream until it disappears in a pile of boulders that look like they'd fallen from the ceiling. Now what?

Let's take a break, Sky suggests. *Some of these rocks look almost comfortable.* She takes her pack off and sits down on a smooth rock with a sigh. It amazes me that she isn't projecting anxiety. Not a trace of fear comes from her.

Why aren't you afraid, Sky? I ask. In fact, why am I not panicking right about now?

I don't have the energy to be afraid. She pulls four granola bars out of her pack and hands them out to us. We put the wrappers in our own packs to discard later.

What's that? I hear Pax's sudden alarm in his mental voice.

Voices, Storm replies. *Quick, behind the rocks, then turn your lamps off. We need to be as still as we can. We know those aren't the Watchers.*

I strain my ears but only hear a deep murmur interrupted by a higher tone every now and then. We sit in complete darkness, and I'm thankful we have our mental link. The voices move closer and we can soon identify the gruff rumble of Dracan voices and, surprisingly, two human females. They're still too far away, and the acoustics echo too much, to make out what they're saying.

Does that sound like Marla? Sky asks. I feel her surprise.

It sounds like her and her mother, Pax answers. *Max identified her voice to us that day in the tunnels under Hunter's woods. She was with the Dracans then, too.*

It's Marla. Storm's agreement carries an undertone of rage. *After all we did for them; they're still working with those monsters.*

We don't know that for sure, Pax reminds him. *They could be here under duress.*

Storm remains silent. I agree with Pax. We should wait and see, but I secretly hope they all get lost in the tunnels. That's not likely since the Dracans have the means to blast their own.

They're still heading in our direction, and soon I can make out their words. "We split up and search the tunnels from this cavern," a Dracan says gruffly. He says something in an eerily sibilant language, probably to the other Dracans in the group, and then speaks again in English, "Woman, you come with me."

"Max and I will search in this direction," Marla announces. Max? What's he doing down here?

They don't move quietly, thank God, and we hear them scurry off in different directions. When the cavern is again silent, I take a chance and peek over the top of the boulder I'm crouched behind, only to let out a mental screech.

Jewel, what's wrong? Pax can't see me but his hand finds my shoulder and pulls me down.

They're here, I say frantically, my heart pounding so loudly I'm sure my friends can hear it in my thoughts. *Right here!*

Just then a cone of light from a flashlight reaches Storm, a couple of boulders away. The rock he's behind shoots into the air and stops for a split second, long enough for us to see it's about to drop on top of Max.

"Wait!" Sky's voice stops him and the rock, as big as a Volkswagen bug, hangs there.

"Tell me why I shouldn't crush the two of you." Storm's voice is full of a dark menace.

"You'll never get out of here without us," Marla says almost casually. I hear a tiny quiver in her voice, but her attitude projects fearless arrogance, as usual.

"We may never get out of here at all," Sky says. "If we don't find and fix that artifact, nothing matters anyway. We're all dead."

"What are you talking about?" Max's face is deathly white in the glow of his flashlight, now shaking so hard that Marla grabs it out of his hand and shoots him a disgusted look. Storm lowers the boulder back to the ground and sits on it, and Max switches his headlamp on.

He asks, "What do you mean we're all dead if you don't find it?"

Marla answers, "We don't have time for them to explain, Max. We have to get them to the artifact before Shaula and his crew find it. If they grab it before these guys do their thing, they're right. We're all dead."

"Do you know where it is?" Pax asks.

"Yes," Marla says. "The Watchers told me before... Never mind. They told me how to get to it."

"Why? Why did they tell you and not us?" Sky sounds like she's about to cry.

I feel Storm's rage flowing off her in rough, quick surges. She can't help sending it my way because it's too much for her to control. Pax wraps his arms around her, but it isn't helping. I want to slap Storm for putting her through this. He's hurting her and I'll bet he doesn't know it.

"Calm down, Storm," I shout and clap my hands over my mouth. Did the Dracans hear that?

"The entrance to the passage you want is near. Are you coming or not?" Marla starts walking back along our path. "Tie Max onto your rope, and Max, douse the light when you're secure. I don't need light to lead you."

Max does as he's told and grabs the back of her jacket before he turns his headlamp off. Marla's already turned off the flashlight. The darkness is so thick; I can't see my hand directly in front of my nose.

"How do you see in this?" I ask her.

"It's one of my gifts," she answers.

After a couple of minutes, I see the glow of the fish in the stream until Marla leads us off the path. The only sound other than the flowing water is scuffling feet and the occasional patter of a dislodged pebble as we blindly follow her through twists and turns. Then the echo of the stream is swallowed up when we enter a narrow tunnel.

"Max, you can turn your headlamp on," she tells him. "His will be sufficient," she tells us, and she's right. We can touch the walls on both sides of the tunnel, and the boys' heads nearly brush the ceiling. The passageway twists and turns until we see light coming from an opening ahead.

"This is it," she announces. "Max and I can't go any farther. The Watchers told me a barrier at the cave entrance will only let those who are authorized by the artifact to get through."

"Do you mean the Dracans can't enter, either?" Storm asks.

"Not through the entrance," she answers. "They have other ways. You'll find the artifact in there. We'll tell the Dracans we didn't find anything when we see them again." At that, she helps Max untie from our rope and the two of them leave.

"We're here," Sky says. "Let's do this."

FORTY-SIX

SKY

Jewel enters the cavern first. If there's a barrier, as Marla said, it gives us no resistance. The cave is filled with light. We release ourselves from the rope and stand there, taking it all in. We don't see anything resembling a tetrahedron.

"Do you hear that?" Storm asks, keeping his voice to a near whisper. I feel it, a low thrumming sound that causes my skin to tingle. Strange.

The cavern is dome-shaped, nearly round in circumference. We follow the trail to a curved wall of columns, where stalactites and stalagmites have joined to form massive pillars fused together side by side. The path leads along the wall, and we walk until we come to an opening where a pillar has been cut out; and there it is. Smack in the middle of the chamber, surrounded by a natural barrier, it hangs from nothing, spinning erratically as if it's off balance.

The glowing object generates all the light in the cavern. I can barely look at it, but Jewel's eyes are glued to it. When I become more accustomed to the bright light, I notice it's made of four equilateral triangle faces that are joined together at four vertex points. Each face is lined with a bronze metallic frame. It's smaller than I imagined. Each side is no more than three feet long. How does something so small affect an entire planet? I wonder how many others are hidden around the earth.

Jewel reaches out and snaps her hand back, as if stung. *That's what I thought*, she tells us. *It's protected by some sort of energy field. I see colors I've never seen before swirling around in there, but they're contained in a globe of energy.*

How do we get in to fix it? Storm asks.

There's a narrow pathway along the inside of the pillar wall that allows us to walk around the artifact and its invisible globe. I sense a trickle of pain and fear that doesn't belong to any of us. It's different from the emotional signatures of my brother and friends; alien. Since I can't feel the emotions of the Allarans or Dracans, I wonder if it's coming from the artifact itself. I notice Pax sniffing.

This thing is emitting some sort of pheromone, he says. *It's not like anything I've smelled before, and it's faint.* We walk around it again, slowly, searching for a way to get to the tetrahedron.

Here, he says. *The scent is trickling from here.*

We stop and Jewel exclaims, *I see a tendril of color leaking out. Could there be a crack in the energy field?*

I let my senses roam over the outside of the field and find it. I tell the others, *I don't know how, but the thing has emotions, and I feel them coming from this area.* I wave my hand over an area directly in front of me, careful not to touch the energy field I can't see.

Storm steps close to me and gently nudges me aside. "Let me try to break it," he says aloud. "If I can focus into the crack, I might be able to widen it."

"If you do that," Pax answers, "it might shatter."

"Let's hope that if it does, the artifact doesn't shatter with it. I see no other option, Pax. Do you?"

I send up a silent prayer. If God put it here and we're supposed to fix it, then God should protect it, shouldn't he? For the first time I feel as if my faith depends on the answer to that question.

I see Storm's eyes grow distant as he focuses on getting into the crack with his telekinesis. I take his hand when I notice sweat breaking out on his forehead. Jewel takes his other hand and Pax takes hers. We lend Storm our strength as best we can.

A loud crackling sound precedes the explosion that lifts me off my feet and throws me against the pillar behind me. My head bounces off the wall and slams into the floor; I lay there in a daze. What just happened? As soon as I can move, I look up, afraid we've lost the artifact. It's still there, but the wobble is more pronounced. We have to move now.

"Storm! Pax! Jewel! Get up! It's about to fall." I stagger to my feet and move from one to the other, shaking them and helping them sit. They're conscious, but dazed. Storm is the first to his feet and he stares at the object. I take a quick look as I help Jewel get up. It's definitely slowing.

A wave of confusion washes over me, followed by a sense of wonder coming from the artifact. *It's sentient*, I think to the others. For some reason I feel mental speech is more appropriate right now than using our voices.

I feel it too, Jewel says, her own wonder evident in her thought.

It wants us to touch it, Pax chimes in. *I don't know how I know that, but it must be the way we can help it.*

There's our answer, then, Storm says, matter-of-factly. *I'll stop the spin and we'll lay hands on it, like good little Christians, and it'll be healed. Then maybe we can get out of here and go back to our real lives.*

How did I miss feeling Storm's anger? I push as much peace and love as I can toward him and feel him rebuff it. It's nearly impossible for me to break through to someone who won't let go of their rage. I try again, and again he stops it. My heart aches and I realize I won't reach him with emotions alone. Will we be able to fix the artifact if he's still so angry? We have no choice but to try.

Once again we link hands as Storm concentrates on slowing the spin without dropping it to the ground. I don't know how we know it, but once it stops, it will no longer be suspended.

Soon we can make out the carvings on each of the faces. They match the symbols on Sequoia's blanket; the four figures surrounded by the earth and the sign for love on one face; the moon, arrow and serpent on another; the coyote, star and butterfly on the third; and the sun of hope on the fourth.

Storm finally gets it to stop moving and holds it in place. We quickly approach it. I'm drawn to the side with the love sign. I see Jewel reach for the coyote and butterfly. Pax gingerly touches the side with the moon and serpent, which leaves the side with hope for Storm.

As we touch it, I feel it tremble and a low vibrating sound comes from its center. It feels warm to the touch, but I get the sense that something is missing. Storm stands next to me, and he isn't touching the artifact.

Storm? I ask.

I can't, he says. *It won't let me touch it.*

"Oh, Storm," I whisper so that only he can hear me. "Don't you know we love you? I love you. You can do this."

His head whips around to me and his eyes are glittering amber. I see them soften. "What did you say?" he whispers back.

Just then the soft vibrations from the artifact increase sharply and it's suddenly shaking under our hands. The floor jerks and pebbles on the stone pathway clatter and roll into each other. Light from the artifact bounces off crystals imbedded in the pillars and I feel a sound building in the ground under the soles of my boots before my ears hear it.

"Hurry, Storm! Touch the thing before we're all goners!" Pax shouts.

I grab Storm's hand and slam it against the carving on his side of the artifact, and I hold it there. Jewel, on his other side, grabs hold of his free hand and presses it with hers against her carving. With her other hand she covers Pax's and he reaches around and covers mine on my carving. It's a bit awkward because of the artifact's shape, but we're able to touch both the artifact and complete a circle of hands at the same time, all while managing to stay on our feet on the shaking ground.

The shaking stops and our ears ring in the sudden silence. The artifact grows warmer under my hands, and the carving in front of me glows with a soft golden light.

Joy fills me and I want to dance and sing and shout with it. I feel a gentle push away from the tetrahedron and we all step back at the same time, letting it go. It begins a slow spin and sends out a wave of love and gratitude, and then it pulls back into itself and begins to hum as its spin accelerates.

Storm taps on his wristband and I know he's tapping my number for a private conversation. *Did you mean what you said before?*

FORTY-SEVEN

STORM

I wait for Sky's answer, afraid I must have misunderstood her; and also afraid she meant what she said. I can't stay cold around her. What will this do to me, if I give in to my feelings for her?

Friends love each other, don't they? Brothers and sisters love each other. She did say 'we' before she said 'I.' I've almost convinced myself she meant that kind of love when she reaches up and places a hand on each side of my face.

Her eyes are oceans and I'm drowning in them. Fire burns low in my belly and heat travels up my chest and into my face. My heart pounds so loudly I'm sure she can hear it. She rises to her tiptoes, pulls my face down to hers and kisses me. Her soft lips move against mine and I pull her close and taste the sweetness of her mouth. Not friends, then. Thank God, not friends.

I hear Pax clear his throat behind me. "That's my sister you're holding there, buddy."

Sky waves him off, and pulls away from me. Her eyes glisten with unshed tears. "We need to find a way out," she says. In my head I hear her say, *every word. I meant every word.*

Jewel is entranced watching the spinning object. I disconnect with Sky and tap in the connection with everyone. *What do you see?* I ask her.

The colors are weaving a ball around it. It's slowly rebuilding its energy field. I've never seen so many colors.

We'd better go. Pax seems anxious to leave, and then I feel it too. He looks at me and I know we're in trouble. The ground is vibrating again.

A blast of sound comes from outside the wall of columns and the ground shakes with the force of an explosion. We rush to the opening and out into the cavern, dodging debris falling from the ceiling. When it stops, a group of Dracans emerges from a tunnel they blasted into the cavern. They stand there, seven of them with weapons pointed at us, and their leader steps forward.

"Thank you for repairing our prize," he says and grins, baring his crocodile teeth.

Rage flares in me. I am going to kill him. I feel Sky trying to calm me. *Not now*, I say, glancing at her. *I need this.* She nods, but I feel a wave of sadness before she quickly snatches it back. I'll make it up to her, I swear it.

I find several loose boulders behind the reptilian creatures and lift them high above their heads. When I let them go, three hit their targets, knocking them flat to the ground. Three down, four to go. The leader fires in my direction and I pull Sky down as I hit the floor. The air above my head sizzles and I hear a boom on the other side of the cavern where the light beam hit. Pax and Jewel take cover behind a pile of rocks.

Keep them occupied, he says. *I'll see if I can get behind them.*
What about their weapons? I ask.
Remember our training, Pax reminds me. In a fight, his bare hands and feet can be lethal weapons.

I pick up every loose rock I find and fling it at them. They blast at the barrage of stones flying at them from everywhere at once. I see two more drop to the floor and I hope they're down for good. I don't see the one crouched behind a stalagmite taking careful aim at me.

I feel the heat of the blast that just misses my face and see Pax take the reptilian down. He makes short work of it, but now the leader, the last one standing, is alerted to his presence.

The Dracan aims at the ceiling above our heads and fires, turns and quickly aims above where Jewel is hiding, fires again, and then spins to confront Pax. That's all I see before the ceiling collapses around me and something hits my head with enough force to knock me out.

"Storm! Storm, wake up," I hear Sky's voice choking on tears and open my eyes. The light from her headlamp slowly comes into focus, and so does a throbbing pain in my head. I press my hand to the source of the pain and feel something sticky. I wonder where my headlamp is.

"How bad is it?" I croak. Dust and gravel clog my throat. She hands me a water bottle and I drink a little too quickly. She helps me sit up and bend forward to cough it up.

"You're alive." Pax's voice sounds like he's full of cotton. He's on a boulder next to me with his knees drawn up, elbows on his knees, holding a flashlight in one hand and covering his face with the other. He's the picture of dejection.

Even more than the pain from my damaged head, I feel a heavy darkness. Wait. Why is it so dark in here? "Where's Jewel?" I ask. Sky breaks down sobbing and Pax picks up a rock and throws it with force against a stalagmite.

"Where is she?" I struggle to get to my feet and nearly fall back down. My legs are weak and my head swims with dizziness. How long have I been out? Leaning against the boulder Pax is on, I hit him on the back. "Answer me!"

He whips around, fists clenched and the rage and grief on his face make my blood run cold. Icy fear grips my heart.

"Gone, Storm!" he shouts. "She's gone!"

I can barely get the word out past the lump in my throat, "Dead?"

"No! I don't know. Maybe," he sounds hollow. "Sky doesn't feel her and she isn't in the link. We can't reach her."

"The artifact is missing, too," Sky says. Except for the small circles of light from the flashlight and headlamp, we're in total darkness. The light from the artifact is gone.

Did we come here for nothing? Is the planet going to die after all?

"Have you searched the cavern to see if she's hurt somewhere?"

Sky answers for both of them. "We came to a while ago, Storm, and searched everywhere we could as soon as I realized I can't feel her. We'll need help and more light to do a more thorough exploration, but we covered the artifact chamber as well as the area where we hid. We knew the tetrahedron was gone when we woke up in darkness. Pax says there's no scent of death in here. They took her, Storm. They took both of them."

I hear a faint sound coming from the Dracan tunnel. "Let's go get her." I use rocks and Pax's boulder to pull myself up, determined to follow them up that tunnel.

"Wait, Storm," Pax says. "They're long gone. That sound is something or someone else. Let's find cover closer to the tunnel and wait."

We hunker down behind the three boulders I dropped on the Dracans. Their bodies are not there, so either they survived or their reptilian buddies carried them out. I hope it was the latter. I wish them all dead.

The noises grow louder and we see a faint light bobbing around a bend in the tunnel. The sounds give way to men's voices, and I recognize Sheriff Green's. He calls our names and Sky answers, "In here, Sheriff."

Wolf is the first one out, and as soon as he spots me, he runs to me and catches me in a strong hug. "Storm, are you alright?" I can't answer and for the first time since my parents died, I break down and sob. He lowers us to the floor where we sit until the wave of grief, pain and rage subsides and I can talk again.

When I finally look up, I see Dylan with one arm around Pax and the other around Sky, talking quietly. Charles and Sheriff Green are on the ground, hunched over, as if in pain. Pax and his dad straighten and start walking back up the tunnel.

"We should all get going," the sheriff says. "There's nothing more we can do here. I'll send my men down with equipment to do a more thorough search, but if Pax is right, they won't find anyone here."

FORTY-EIGHT

SKY

I sit on the porch swing at Jewel's house, warm in my down jacket, and wait for the O'Connells to arrive. The headmaster, pastor, and other tribal elders are inside with my parents and Charles and Analiese, drinking coffee and eating some of the piles of food brought over by friends and neighbors. My folks have been inundated with food, as well, and so have the O'Connells.

Our community brought us our Thanksgiving and Christmas meals. It's their way of showing gratitude for the help we extended during and after the flood, and their kindness in turn has sustained us in our grief. We did our best to celebrate with them, but a pall of sadness still hangs over us.

The ache in my heart, amplified by everyone else's pain, is nearly as acute as the moment when I realized Jewel was taken. I want to send comfort, but I'm exhausted with it. Pax is still inconsolable. His despair is a black hole, sucking all joy from everyone around him.

Wolf and Sequoia drive up, with Storm in the back seat. I wonder if I'll ever see him smile again. I long to comfort him, but he's distanced himself. I long for him to put his arms around me to comfort me, but it's obvious he doesn't feel the same for me as I do for him. His wall is thick and cold, pushing me away. I worry about Storm. Will he survive this? Does he love Jewel the way my brother does?

The sheriff arrives last in his SUV with the rack of lights on top. I almost wish they were turned on, if only to see light and color again. Grief turns everything gray. Sheriff Green is grieving, too.

Max is missing, and the official story is that he disappeared in the flood. His father knows the truth, though. Max and Marla were with the Dracans when they stole the artifact and Jewel, and now they're gone. We will never see any of them again, and the world will end.

In fact, the news hasn't been that bad these last three months. Construction on the new road over the gap made by the sliding mountain is nearly complete. The weather over the continental United States and Canada has been mostly average for the season, and there haven't been any earthquakes to report. Wherever the artifact is, it seems to be working.

I greet Storm, who nods and follows his folks into the house. I follow, too, hang up my jacket and find a spot to sit against the wall in the living room. The adults sit around our dining room table talking quietly. I rest my head on my folded arms on top of my bent knees.

Pax slides down next to me. He taps his wristband for the first time since the cavern. *I'm sorry I've been so distant, Sky.* I glance at him and he's a mirror image of me; knees up, head down on his arms.

I understand, Pax. I miss her, too. I wish you'd let me send you some peace.

It's like half of me has been ripped away.

I look at Storm sprawled on the couch, arm flung over his face. *He's hurting, too.*

Pax glances at him and then looks at me. I hate the desolation I see in his eyes. I hate the waves of grief that batter me from all sides and reduce me to a pool of anguish. I can't help either of them.

I see Storm tap on his wrist and he joins the link. *I knew Marla was up to something when she and Max left. She must have told them where we were.*

I'm not so sure, I say. *I've replayed it endlessly in my mind. When we rescued her and her mom from their cabin, she told us she owed us one. I think she repaid us in the cave when she led us to the artifact chamber. Why would she turn around and betray us? It doesn't make sense.*

Pax chimes in. *Does any of it make sense? The Watchers told us the Dracans want to trade the artifacts for a way to get them home to their planet. They're the enemy. Some Dracans don't want to leave and know that the artifacts are Earth's hope for survival. They've allied themselves with the Allarans. The bad ones got what they came for, so why take Jewel?*

And why involve Max, for that matter, Storm says. *I can't imagine them having any use for him, unless it's for food.*

Oh, stop, Storm! I'll never get that image out of my head now. Oh, God, what are they doing to Jewel? My body is ice cold with dread. Is she dead or alive? If she's alive, does she wish she's dead? Lord, if only we knew anything at all.

"Kids, come on over here and get something to eat," Mom calls. We obediently get up and grab plates, but none of us really has an appetite and we barely make a dent in the amount of food on the counters. I sit between Pastor John and Dad.

"I know the kids have completed the required credits to graduate," Pastor John is saying, "but school would be good for them. They should be around other kids; get involved in sports or some other activities. There's nothing more for them to do with the artifact, and it's been three months since the incident in the cave."

Dad speaks up, "They train with me, John. They're involved in karate, and they work well together. Coral and I are willing to have them continue their education at our house. They're all taking college-level courses as it is, and we are professors."

The boys and I remain silent while the adults decide the course of our immediate future for us. We don't care. Life will never be the same without Jewel.

After we eat, the boys and I get our jackets and go back to the porch. I take Jewel's favorite spot on the swing, Pax sinks into an Adirondack chair, and Storm sits on the top step. The cold air feels good.

I want to turn my feelings off for a while, but how do I do that when the people I love most are hurting so much?

I can almost hear Jewel's voice in my head. *Antiss.* Wait. What was that? What does antiss mean? Why would I imagine her saying something so weird?

Storm jumps to his feet. Pax pushes out of the chair. *Antiss.* There it is again, now clearly her voice.

Jewel! Where are you? Pax's mental shout is louder in my head than his voice would have been. Storm echoes him. *Where are you, Jewel?*

Antiss. Her voice fades away on the last syllable and I feel her leave the link.

"She's alive," I say, and my heart lifts. "Pax, go tell her parents! She's alive!"

My brother grabs my hands and pulls me out of the swing into a tight hug. "Thank God," he whispers into my hair, and I feel our normal connection for the first time since Jewel was taken. Peace washes over me, and he turns to the door and disappears into the house.

Storm sinks back to his seat on the top step. He stares over the meadow and narrows his eyes. I see his jaw clench and his shoulders tense. His pain and rage rip into me.

"We'll find her, by God, and when we do, I'm going to tear those monsters apart one by one."

I feel my heart shatter in a million splinters. Our Storm is raging, and he's in love with Jewel.

FORTY-NINE

Jewel is alive, but where? I wonder if the Allarans know where she is. Is there a way to contact them? I get up and go inside. Maybe Charles can signal them with his lab equipment. We need some answers, and soon.

It looks like everyone has gone to Charles's office for a meeting. I head downstairs and hear Pax's raised voice. "We heard her! She's alive, and we are going after her."

"How will you find her?" Charles shakes his head and rubs his hand through his hair. I imagine he and Analiese haven't slept much, worrying about their daughter.

"I have an idea," I say from the doorway, "but I'm not sure how to go about it."

"What is it, Sky?" My dad looks tired, too. No one seems excited to learn that Jewel spoke to us. I wonder if they're afraid to hope.

"Does anyone know how to contact the Allarans? We haven't heard from them since we fixed the artifact, but they might know exactly where she is."

Sequoia says, "I was once able to communicate with the Watchers, but not since the artifact was stolen. They may not have survived the attack you told us about. I will try to send my thoughts to the Allarans, but I haven't contacted them before."

Storm comes in, stands next to me near the door and says, "What if we form a link through the wristbands and we call them together? The combined focus might reach them."

Dad looks thoughtful. "You, Pax, and Sky link up. We'll activate the emergency link, and include Charles and Analiese. That should put all of our heads together, so to speak. Before we do, will we all speak at once, or will one of us act as spokesman, or spokeswoman?"

"Sequoia has experience calling the Watchers," Wolf says. "Perhaps we can send her our energy somehow."

"Jewel told me that when we were in Vega's ship the first time," I tell them, "she opened a link with her dad wide enough for him to see what she saw and hear what she heard. If we open our minds, maybe Sequoia can use our energy to send a beam of thought to Vega."

"The *first* time you were on Vega's ship?" Mom asks. Nothing gets by her. Our folks still don't know that we went on that rescue mission to get Wolf and Sequoia from the Dracans. I guess we'll have to tell them we've been in the Allaran ship more than once, after we do this.

Sheriff Green, the other tribal elders and the pastors are listening to this conversation with a great deal of interest. I forgot that they didn't know about the wristbands or what we can do with them.

"If there's a chance that my son was taken alive, he could be where Jewel is," Sheriff Green wipes his hand across his face. He's paler than usual. Losing Max has been terrible for him.

Chief O'Brian adds, "You do whatever you can to find the kids, and I'll see that you have the resources you need to do the job. The Cherokee are at your service. You kids have done something I would have said was impossible. You may have saved the planet, at least for now."

The elders nod and talk in soft murmurs until Dad says, "Let's do this."

I tap my wristband. Pax and Storm do the same, and I see my parents tap theirs. *Mom? Dad?* I start a roll call and everyone checks in.

Now, open your minds to Sequoia, I instruct them. I've never done it and don't know how to teach them what Jewel did, but it does feel natural to open my mind. I feel a stronger connection to everyone else. In fact, I share their wonder that we're actually creating a deeper link. I feel Sequoia drawing strength from us and growing stronger.

I sense her gather our energy around her, and my soul vibrates when she calls, *VEGA!* The name resonates and pushes outward like a beacon of sound.

We hear and we come, came the answer, clear and vibrant.

One by one, we go upstairs, put on our jackets and go outside. If the Allarans are willing to lead us to Jewel and Max, we might have a chance to rescue them.

The silver ship hovers over the meadow, and Vega waits. Storm, Pax and I walk forward while the others hang back.

"Star Children," his silken voice electrifies me, but his power to attract me is gone. I silently thank Storm for that, or at least my feelings for him.

"We believe we have found where the Dracans have taken Jewel, but where she is we cannot go, and it will be nearly impossible for you to rescue her."

Pax's voice rings with confidence when he responds, "Nothing will stop us, Vega. We'll succeed. We have to."

"And I swear I will tear those lizards limb from limb," Storm declares.

"First, you must find and then rescue her, Storm. As for destroying them, you will see that things are not always what they seem. Beware of your temper and use wisdom, or you may destroy yourself and all those you love."

The emotions I feel from Storm thrash and whip around wildly. I'm afraid he'll tear himself apart with the violence of his anger. I look at Pax and my fear nearly knocks me to my knees. He is just as angry as Storm.

"There is one more thing, Star Children. After you rescue Jewel, you must also find and repair the next artifact. You have repaired the one, but that has merely bought us a little time. The continued existence of your world and ours depends on you."

"You said you have an idea where she is," Pax says. "Where is she?"

Vega looks at him gravely and says something I didn't expect to hear. How is it possible?

"To find Jewel, you must go to Atlantis."

Made in the USA
Charleston, SC
13 April 2016